THE HEART OF THE MOON

With Bonus Story 'The Dry Season'

PUBLISHER'S ACKNOWLEDGEMENTS

Immanion Press would like to thank Jeremy Brett and his staff at the Cushing Memorial Library & Archives, Texas A&M University, for a providing a scanned archive copy of the novella 'The Heart of the Moon'. Thanks also to Allison Rich, who administers Tanith Lee's online bibliography 'Daughter of the Night', for her assistance in sourcing the novella and proof-reading the finished book.

THE HEART OF THE MOON

With Bonus Story 'The Dry Season'

Tanith Lee

IMMANION PRESS
Stafford England

The Heart of the Moon, by Tanith Lee © 2nd edition 2020. First published in *Winter Moon*; Luna Books, Harlequin Enterprises (Australia), 2005.
'The Dry Season', first published in *Dreams of Dark and Light* Arkham House, 1986

Cover Art and Design by Danielle Lainton
Interior layout by Storm Constantine
Interior Illustrations by Danielle Lainton

ISBN: 978-1-912815-05-0
IP0156

Author Site:
Daughter of the Night: An Annotated Tanith Lee Bibliography:
http://www.daughterofthenight.com/

Facebook Page for Tanith Lee's readers: Paradys Forum - Daughter of the Night - Tanith Lee

An Immanion Press Edition
www.immanion–press.com
info@immanion–press.com

INTRODUCTION

Dear Reader,

The heart of the moon is, of course, the heart of a cool, strong and self-controlled woman. In this case, Clirando. She wears a 'mask' because she's been hurt. And because she is tough, she challenges what hurt her, and drives it off.

But most of us know there are things that, discard or deny them as we may, leave their marks on us, like the scratches of a lion. Some fade, some scar. The *scars* are still there to be looked at long, long after.

I wanted very much to find a way to free my character from her hurt. She deserved that. But like most of the ones I write about, she, or others in this tale, told me how her freedom would come about. She needed not only new light, but the means to confront the shadows. When Zemetrios entered the story and showed his worth, the core of the narrative began to flame – the fire-heart was being refuelled.

In fact, I first saw the heroine's name in a dream, written across a white moon above a dark isle. It's a kind of play on words, too, I believe. Clir-an-do:

Clear and do.

Tanith Lee

PROLOGUE
LIGHTNING

The moon's face is cold, but her heart is full of fire—how else could she give such light?

The night that lightning struck the Temple of the Maiden – that was the night she found them. Clirando would never have suspected the warrior goddess Parna of such harsh melodrama. Though justice, of course, was partly her province. It seemed she had wanted Clirando to see and to know. Perhaps she had expected Clirando to behave differently after it had happened.

The narrow streets of Amnos were moon-and-torch lit, and people were shouting and running up toward the Sacred Mount, where stood the temples of the Father and Parna the Maiden. Smoke and a thin flame still sizzled from her roof, and the sea-washed air was full of the reek of scorching stone.

But by the time Clirando reached the lower terrace, men were already on the tiles, girls, too, from the various female warrior bands. Clirando saw two of her own command, Oani and Erma, busy there.

She shouted to them. "Are you safe?"

"Yes, safe, Cliro. But come up..."

One of the men, no less than the architect Pholis, swathed in his bed gown, called down, "Use the stairs! No more swarming on ropes here, the roof is damaged."

So Clirando and several others ran up the final terrace and in from the side court.

There were guest rooms off the court. Priests and others used them, if they were on duty that night at the temple.

Almost everybody had come out. They stood around the tank of crystal water under the fig tree, talking, shaking their heads, some offering prayers.

Two people were late, however, leaving a room.

As Clirando walked into the court – yawning, she afterward recalled, for the levin-bolt had woken her from sleep like most of the town – she saw them. One was Araitha, her closest friend. The other dark-haired Thestus.

Clirando knew them both so well that for a long moment it did not startle her to see them there. She was pleased, very probably. Her best friend, as well as her lover, Thestus, both of whom would be excellent at assisting on the roof.

Even with his hand slipping from Araitha's shoulder... even with the way Araitha suddenly drew aside from him, her eyes blank with far too many emotions to show.

And his rasp of guilty laugh.

"Ha – Cliro. Are you going up, too? That was a strike and no mistake. A wonder the temple withstood…"

Behind the two of them, the curtain of the little room had been drawn back, to show a dishevelled bed, narrow but still wide enough for the pair of slender and hard-muscled figures who had chosen to couch there together. A flagon of wine stood on the floor. In the grey-red moon-and-torch mixing of the light, it gleamed in a horrible way, blinking and winking at Clirando like the centre of an evil eye: *Didn't you guess, girl*? it seemed to say. *Didn't you know*?

Clirando walked past the water tank and met Thestus and Araitha at the door of the cell and pushed them both back inside. They let her do this, not resisting.

Thestus was taller than she, but Araitha was her own height. Araitha with her beer-brown eyes and long, dark golden hair. Thestus had always honestly praised that hair. And other things. Araitha's warrior skills, her musical gift with lira and tabor. Clirando, Araitha's sister-friend since they had been six years old in the training courts of the temple, was always happy when others praised Araitha.

As for Thestus, he had come to the Father Temple, a warrior, with his own band of twenty men, only two years before. He had singled Clirando out inside three days, as she had him. Since the Spring Festival they had been lovers. Parna never minded such liaisons. Her warriors were also allowed love, and to make children, if they wished.

Clirando shook her own long brown hair over her shoulders and looked at him. Then she looked at Araitha.

Neither of them spoke.

Thestus's mouth locked shut as if a key had turned behind his lips.

It was Araitha who laughed now and said, scattering her words light as beads, "Oh, Cliro. It means nothing. We only – only for a moment. That was all."

"Liar."

"Cliro – what could it matter? We both love you. Do you…" she threw back her head, defiant "…grudge me a little pleasure?"

Always her way. Attack was defence to Araitha.

"I grudge you this."

Thestus opened his locked lips and spoke to Araitha. "Don't try to reason with her. We both know what she can be like when she loses her self-control."

Cliro turned and slapped him stingingly across the mouth.

He swung aside with a curse, was already reaching for the dagger lying in its sheath on the floor. Araitha made a noise. Cliro kicked Thestus's hand away, then kicked Thestus full in the chest so he fell back bruisingly on his well-formed butt.

"No," said Cliro. "Soon but not yet, sweetheart."

"Cliro…" said Araitha.

Clirando no longer liked the sound of her name from her friend's beautiful mouth. The mouth was very red and swollen from Thestus's kisses tonight. Maybe that was why the name of *Cliro* sounded wrong.

"Be quiet, you bitch. Both of you. I'll issue the challenge now, so you know. In seven days at first light, before the Maiden. First you, I think, Thestus, for the shorter time I've known you – if ever I knew you at all. A little later for you, Araitha, you filthy slut."

"I am no…"

"*You are a slut*. You are a *traitor*. To me. Him I hate. But *you* I hate the most. I called you friend."

Araitha began to cry, like any soft merchant's wife.

Clirando turned, her own eyes burning. She stalked

out and across the court, where the others standing there, who had seen most and heard all of it, murmured together.

She knew that anyone, other perhaps than some great sage, would have felt shocked pain and anger. But aside from her personal hurt, this very publicly witnessed betrayal showed her own judgement up poorly. No one could fail to be aware she had been in ignorance until tonight. Clirando was a commander. In no respect could she be seen to have been stupid.

She thought now, in horror, that, blind to their antics, she might well have trusted them beside her in battle – and possibly been unwise in that, too. Had their desire proved so irresistible, honour demanded they should have told her to her face. But they had deceived her, as if she were some silly woman reared only for the house.

Clirando did not go up to the lightning-blasted roof. "Forgive me," she said to the goddess, in the private shrine beside the main hall. Amber lamplight starred the goddess's calm face. Polished marble etched and dressed with gold, her eyes were two green stones. Clirando also had green eyes – Thestus had said they were green as leaves of the bay tree. "I can't help mend your roof, Maiden. I'm shaking like some fool before her first skirmish. Pardon me."

The calm face looked down at hers.

"I will meet both Araitha and Thestus individually in the war-court. Before the whole town. I think you allowed me to see what those two had done to me, to find them out. I'll punish them. Oh, not a fight to the death. But I'll shame them both. They'll lose their places in Amnos and go far away. Where I need never look at them again. Do you allow it, Lady?"

Above, there came a faint rushing – tiles dislodged – and then cries and a crash as they plummeted onto the terraces below.

"Is that disapproval, Lady?"

Parna did not answer. But Clirando had never known her to. It was a formality to ask. Clirando's human course was already set.

She had long thought, though one must respect the gods, one could not expect understanding from them. They gave favours or hurts according to some indecipherable law of their own.

And I am hurt, she thought. *Struck in the heart*.

She would make them pay, her lover, her sister. There was no other road now to peace.

Arguments among the warrior-priests of Parna and the Father were often settled in the war-court, in public duel.

Generally, it was two men who fought. Women tended to settle their disagreements with only their bands to witness. Rarely did a female warrior demand satisfaction of a male in the court, though there had been cases now and then. Clirando had known that aside from the officials and certain priests bound to attend, a lot of Amnos would crowd into the public seats to see.

It had occurred to her that many people had known about Thestus's liaison with Araitha. Some even came to her, subsequent to her finding out, and confessed – among these was Erma from Clirando's own band.

"I never knew if I should tell you, Cliro…"

"You should have."

"I know. But…"

Clirando forgave Erma, who was holding back her tears. She was still young, only fifteen, five years younger than Clirando.

Tuyamel, on the other hand, offered to skin Thestus for Clirando.

"I wouldn't want the skin, thanks, my friend," Clirando said.

Tuy had laughed. "Fair enough. I shall leave it to you, then."

The morning was fine, the sun just torching the east, when Clirando stood on the war-court and faced her former lover across the clean paving.

All around, the crowd sat in respectful silence. There was none of the shouting or merriment that went on when ritual games or war exercises took place here. This was a solemn, fraught occasion.

Clirando had to steel herself, too. She had fought beside Thestus only once in battle – against pirates last fall, blood raining among red leaves at the edges of Amnos's forested shores. But often he and she had exercised together. They knew each other's moves perhaps too well.

She had thought he would try to surprise her. She judged correctly.

The instant the signal came to begin, he dropped onto the ground and came rolling at her like a human hedgehog. As she leaped aside, his short sword whipped out. It cut one of her sandal thongs. Only her reflexes had saved her from much worse.

She tore off both sandals and he, having stood up again, watched her mockingly.

There was contempt in his face. Maybe that was only a mask. Or maybe his looks of love had been the mask.

She had tried very hard not to examine why he had used her as he had, and played her false. Now certainly was not the time for analysis.

Clirando wondered if he had other tricks, and he had.

Having allowed her space to undo her shoes, he lounged idly, paring his nails, so a slight amusement rippled through some of the audience, only to be shushed as improper.

He would not move again to meet her.

She stood waiting.

He stood idling. He began to whistle a popular tune of the town.

"Come on," she said. Her voice carried.

"I'm here if you want me. *You* come on."

She knew it was another trick.

Clirando moved toward him slowly, then suddenly very fast, running as if straight into him – veering at the last second. A fine pinkish powder spurted from his left hand, clouding the air between them. He must have taken it out with the paring knife. It would have been in her face, her eyes, if she had dodged less effectively. Play dirty, then. A bitter smile touched her mouth. He must be scared of her.

From veering, she swung and cut him across the left shoulder. Blood burst like a flower.

With a roar he turned on her.

To her he seemed heavy now, graceless. He had not bothered to prepare for this, only his tricks. She had been practicing every day.

He was a poor warrior. Brave and strong, cunning sometimes. But his skill was not so great. She had thought more highly of him when she had loved him, seeing him through lover's eyes, wanting him to shine.

Inside six minutes more, she had scored him lightly across arms and chest, thighs, and even his back as he went skidding down from a sidelong blow. She did not aim to cripple him. He would need his fighter's trade where he was going, out into the wide world, far from Amnos.

But by then he was a mess, and losing blood, his face pale and congested, ugly, frantic. He was bellowing at her, oaths and blasphemies for which the priests would be setting him a penance. He told her, also, and told the crowd, why he had lost his sexual interest in her. She was too cold, he said. Cold as Moon Isle with its heartless crags. She was too masculine. She had no feminine gifts to match her male ones.

Clirando knew these things were lies, and saw that possibly, in desperation, he was trying to unnerve her that way, and so catch her off guard. She felt nothing by then, only the desire to end the fight. As he lunged, she brought up her blade under his and sent it spinning – to be fair, his sword had grown slippery from his blood – then she punched him clean and square on the point of the jaw. He keeled over and fell with a crash, his already unconscious eyes staring at her all the way down.

The priest and priestess of the court approached and asked if Clirando was satisfied.

"Yes. But one more thing."

"What is it?"

"Let him be sent away."

"You know, Clirando, that he must be. You have disgraced him before the town. He will never fight for Amnos again."

They offered her an interval to rest, then.

Clirando said she would meet Araitha at once.

She believed this would be harder, but in fact when her sister-friend came out, pale and angry and lovely in the broadening rays of the sun, Clirando felt nothing still.

They fought well and without tricks for ten minutes, during which each cut the other.

Clirando thought, *This is too much like play. This is too much like times when we have done this for exercise, and to learn from each other.*

Something came to Clirando then. The terrible rage she had not wanted to feel and, so far, had avoided feeling.

When she loses her self-control, he had said.

Clirando lost it.

Some part of her stood in the air, watching in astonishment as she slashed and hacked at Araitha, who was now falling back before her.

Words tried to boil from Clirando's mouth. She held them in, but they radiated from her eyes she believed, judging by Araitha's face.

Finally, Clirando sprang. She went through the swirl of Araitha's blade – which afterward Clirando found had sliced her left arm from shoulder to elbow. As they tumbled over, she drove her knee into Araitha's midriff, exploding all breath from her body.

Clirando knelt over her vanquished opponent, plucked the sword from Araitha's loose grip and slung it clattering across the court.

"You're done," she hissed.

Araitha had no breath. She sprawled away and curled up on the paving, crowing for air, in the same posture Thestus had adopted when first attacking.

"Clirando, are you satisfied?"

"Yes."

"She too is disgraced. She too will never fight for Amnos again."

A victor might be applauded by the crowd.

The stands were applauding loudly. In the tumult Clirando could hear the battle shouts of her own band.

She did not look, did not acknowledge. She went below to one of the fighters' rooms, was bandaged, drank a pitcher of ale, and fell into a deadly sleep.

Araitha visited Clirando's house three nights later. It was the hour before Araitha's ship was to sail, taking her away to the distant city of Crentis, where she had relatives. Thestus by then was long gone.

Araitha wore a woman's dress and heavy cloak, and her hair was braided with golden ornaments.

She stood staring at Clirando.

Clirando said, "Who let you in?"

"Old Eshti. She doesn't know. She thinks we are still friends."

Above, the dusk was already full of stars over the

little courtyard. A tiny fountain tickled the night with silvery sounds, and leaves rustled in the trees as the house doves settled. Through a lighted door, Eshti the servant woman was already bringing cups of fruit juice and wine.

"Thank you, Eshti," said Clirando. "Put them there."

"Something to warm you. The nights turn colder," said Eshti. "And she, our poor lady-girl, this long journey." Then Eshti went to Araitha and pressed her young hand in two old ones. "Don't fret, dear. You'll be home in Amnos before too long. I'll see the mistress doesn't forget you."

Clirando had not been startled by her servant Eshti's ignorance of what had happened – only glad Eshti, who would have been upset, had not been bothered with it. The market no doubt would have carried the gossip, but Eshti was a little deaf, and besides well-known and liked. It seemed lips were tactfully sealed when she approached.

When the old woman had gone, Clirando found she had dug her sharp nails into her palms. She relaxed her fists.

"Best she doesn't know then," she said. "But tell me, before you go, what you could possibly want from me?"

"To give you something, Clirando."

"I want nothing of yours. How could you think I would?"

"This gift you must take."

"No."

"Yes. I've had it especially worked for you. The ancient women who live in the caves on the mountainside - they helped me fashion it."

Clirando's heart turned to stone.

Witches lived up there, and other mad and dangerous sorts.

She readied herself for one more trick – some poison or assault.

Araitha spoke softly. "I curse you, Clirando. It's nothing much. Your life will be hollow as an emptied jar. Nothing in it but dust. Love may come and go; adventures may come and go. But they will echo in the hollow of you, and they too will become dust. And never again will you sleep. Oh, no. That respite from your thoughts will never be yours – unless some drug gives it to you. All your life, be it short or long, sleepless and empty you shall go."

Clirando shrugged. "You're a fool, Araitha."

Araitha said nothing.

Her face was like a statue's, expressionless and blind. She slipped away out of the courtyard, vanishing from dark to light to darkness in the subtle way of a ghost.

Clirando poured the juice and wine on the ground. They *had* been poisoned, by Araitha's words, her childish, horrible little bane.

Clirando was not afraid.

She spent the evening as she had planned, reading books and scrolls from her father's library. He had been both scholar and soldier and had travelled to many lands.

At the usual hour Clirando went to bed. Coolly, she mused a moment on Araitha's words, but paid them no proper heed. Just as she always normally did, she fell asleep swiftly, and slumbered until morning. She had suspected it was a feeble curse.

The trading ship, the *Lion,* which was to carry Araitha to Crentis, sank in a gale off the unfriendly coasts of Sippini.

All on board were drowned, and the ship herself dragged to the bottom. Only remnants of cargo washing into the port evidenced what had happened.

When news reached Amnos two months after, it was Tuyamel and Vlis who came in person to tell Clirando.

She heard the tidings quietly. When her girls were gone, Clirando threw a pinch of incense into the watch fire of her private shrine.

"Forgive her, Parna. Let her live well in the lands beyond death. Forgive me too for I don't know what I must feel."

That night Clirando dreamed of Araitha, not drowning, nor as she had been in life, but veiled and hidden, passing through a shadow to a light – to a shadow.

When Clirando woke with a start it was still deep night. She lay awake through the rest of it, until dawn showed in the window.

The following night, though tired from exercise, she did not sleep at all.

Her life was active and under her command. She did not think this insomnia could last. But it lasted. Night followed night, sleepless. She grew accustomed to the changing patterns of moon and cloud reflected on the ceiling. Even when exhausted, as she came to be, she lay down to rest at noon, sleep would not come. It fluttered over the room before the cinders of her eyes, brushed her with its wing, and flew far, far off.

Death it seemed had cemented the curse firmly into a place of power. Or, it was Parna's punishment.

Winter entered Amnos. Now was the time of long nights.

Clirando suffered it as best she could. When an alarm rang from the town's brazen gongs, she leaped down the streets leading her band among the other warriors. Pirates were trying their luck again, made hungry by lean weather. They were beaten back into the sea. Clirando's band did well and sustained no casualties.

As the season moved toward spring, Clirando took herself in hand. The physician had already supplied her with an herbal medicine, which scarcely had an effect. Now she gained a stronger one. With its aid, every third or fourth night she was able to sleep two or three hours – though waking always with a heavy head and sickened stomach.

The bane will die away in its own time, like a venomous plant. I must ignore it, which will lessen its hold on me.

She pushed the burden from her, would not think of it by day, and lay reading through the nights.

Strangely, her body, young and fit, acclimatised to sleep loss, even if, on the third or fourth evening without slumber, sometimes she would see phantoms moving under trees or against walls – tricks of her tired eyes. Surely not real?

The priestess she consulted listened carefully to all

Clirando told her. The priestess, who had been a warrior too in her youth, and was now middle-aged and stout, told Clirando gently, "And you have not mourned Araitha."

"No, Mother. I've made offerings to the goddess for her sake and put flowers by the altars in Araitha's name. But I can't mourn. I – I'm angry still. *Disgusted* still."

"Yet you fought her and bested her and ruined her life in Amnos."

"Do you mean I killed her?" Clirando stared. "It was because she had to go away that she died."

"No. It wasn't you who caused her drowning. The sea and the wind did that. But you broke her spirit, Clirando. Why else did she curse you in that way?"

"She could have wished *me* dead."

"I think," said the priestess quietly, "she preferred you to live and suffer. Thestus did not curse you. He didn't care enough – or love enough. But Araitha was your sister. Measure her feeling for you by her last acts."

"What shall I do?"

"Like all of us, Clirando, you can only do what you are able. Do that."

The moon, which by now figured so vividly in Clirando's sleepless nights, began to be important to all the town – indeed to all the known world, from Crentis to Rhoia, and the burning southern deserts of Lybirica.

Every sixteen or seventeen years, through the strange blessing of the gods, there would come seven nights of midsummer when every night the moon would be full: seven nights together of the great white orb, coldly glowing as a disk of purest marble lit from within by a thousand torches.

The last such time had been in Clirando's earliest childhood. She had only the dimmest memory of it, of her mother leading her up among the family on the roof each night to see – and of all the house roofs of Amnos being similarly crowded with people, who let off Eastern firecrackers in spiralling arcs of gold and red. Among Clirando's band, only Erma and Draisis had never seen the seven full moons.

But all of them had heard of the Moon Isle. Even Thestus, come to that. He had compared Clirando to its unlovely rocks when they fought.

The Isle lay out in the Middle Sea, beyond Sippini. It was sacred and secret but, as was also well-known, on every occasion of the Seven Nights, certain persons had to go there, to honour and invoke the moon's power.

Amnos would send its delegation of priests and priestesses. Sometimes others were selected to sail to the Isle. How they were chosen was never made public, and no one was permitted to speak – or ever did so – of what took place upon the island. Nevertheless, or perhaps *because* of the silence, theories abounded. The Isle was full of dangerous and terrible beasts, also of spirits and demons. It was a spot of ultimate ordeal and test—and some of those sent there had not returned.

Clirando herself had never speculated unduly. She had been too busy, too fulfilled in her life.

The same priestess was waiting for her when she

answered the temple's summons and entered the shrine beside the main hall.

In the altar light below the statue of Parna, the dumpy older woman had gained both grace and presence. "I have something to tell you, Clirando."

"Yes, Mother?"

"You, and the six girls of your band, have been selected for an important duty."

"Certainly, Mother. We'll be glad to see to it."

"Perhaps not." The faintest nuance went over the priestess's face. It was an unreadable expression – caused only, maybe, by the flicker of the altar lamp. "You seven are to travel to the Moon Isle."

Clirando felt her heart trip over itself. She swallowed and said, "To the Isle?"

"Yes. You will leave in ten days, in order to be there at the commencement of the Moon Month."

"Mother – this is an honour for us – but none of us have any notion of what we must do when we arrive."

"None have," said the priestess flatly.

"But then—"

"Clirando. This is both an honour for you, as you say, a reward for your valour and care in the past – and a penance. A privilege and a trial. You'll have heard disturbing things of the place, yes?"

"Yes, Mother. I thought most of them fanciful."

"Forget that impression. The Isle is supernatural and may produce anything. It is a place half in this world and half elsewhere. In spots, they say, it opens on the country of the moon itself. For philosophers have decided the moon is not what it appears, a disk, but rather a world, an unlike mirror to our own. Therefore, anticipate magic, and great danger. Sacrifice is common on the Isle. So is death. But too the land is mystical and profound, and from death life may spring. There is a saying, a closed eye may sometimes see more there than one which stares. Do you consent to go?"

"Mother – *I* consent. But my girls..."

"Have no fear for them. They will be safer than you. *You,* Clirando, are the one the isle requires. Human presence on it invokes the power of the moon, her cold fire. But sometimes pain is needed in the process, but not from all."

Clirando felt a shadow fall on her, like a heavy cloak for travelling. Her sleep-starved eyes half glimpsed Araitha suddenly, standing there in the shade behind the goddess's statue, motionless, with face averted.

"This is my true punishment, then."

"You may see it as such," said the priestess. "Or as a chance at salvation. The seas at this time of year are calm as honey. The voyage will last no longer than nineteen days, and perhaps rather less. Go now and tell you band. Pack anything you may need, for battle or for mere existence."

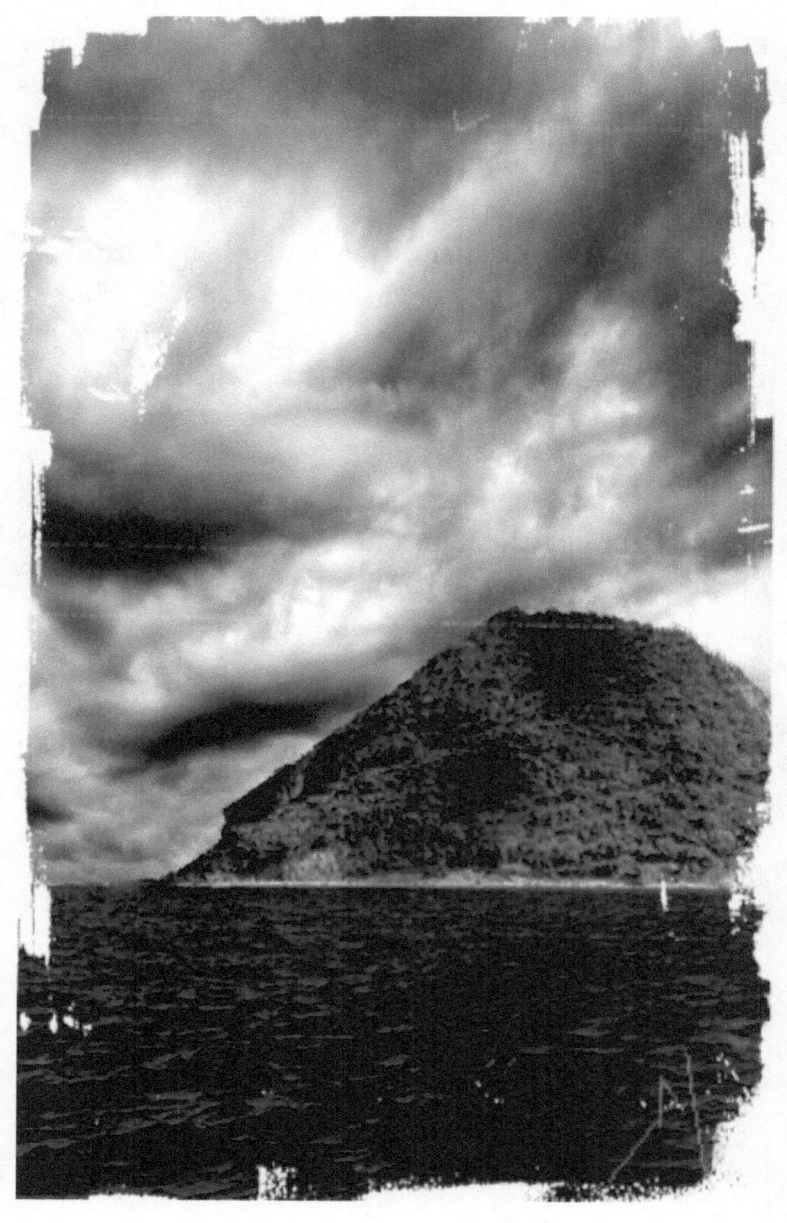

1.

LANDSCAPE

Across night and water, in darkness: the island.

There was no moon tonight. Tomorrow was the moon's First Night.

"Clirando, do you see?"

"I see. The beacons are burning."

High up, the coastal cliffs were gemmed with them, drops of brilliant fire, each one separated from the next by many miles.

They were like eyes, watching, as the boat came in. Nothing else was to be seen, but the luminous rollers of the surf on the shore.

The galley had put them off as soon as the sun set in the Middle Sea. The Isle was visible, a black dot far away. The captain told Clirando the water there was too shallow for his ship, but also no man or woman, unless called or ordered to the Isle, might go in any nearer.

Strong, and aching for action after the slow voyage, the band was quite eager to take up oars and row.

Gradually the sea dulled to a leaden blue and the sky faded like an autumn rose. Great darkness came, scattered with stars. The galley had drawn away.

Briefly the younger girls chattered, excited or unnerved. Then they fell silent as the rest.

The hump of the island grew from the night, always

still blacker, and then the beacons burned out above.

Clirando had been given by the captain a rudimentary map, which showed a way in. They found the entry soon enough. A narrow defile sliced between and below the steep surfaces of the cliffs.

They followed the sea channel and soon the beacons were left behind them. Only starlight then shone like steel on the water.

For perhaps a further quarter of an hour they rowed under the cliff stacks, until the channel opened again into an inner bay.

They drew the boat up across pale shingle.

A statue of an unknown goddess stood there, guarding the beach, her eyes glittering grey zircons.

"Who is she?" whispered Draisis.

Seleti said, "Maut, I think."

"A goddess of the East?" asked Tuyamel. "Do *you* think it's Maut, Cliro?"

Clirando bowed to the goddess. "Maybe. But whoever she is, this is her place. We'll offer some wine when we uncork the skin."

After they had set their fire, the ordinary sounds of arrival and domestic preparation ended. Then each of the women heard, Clirando thought, the vast stillness close about them. It was intense and fur-soft, and fearful, this silence. It had in it a kind of tinsel quivering—noiseless yet always in the ears. They spoke, the women, in hushed tones, eating the cold meats and apples from home, drinking the wine.

Clirando observed them. They were good girls, awed and probably nervous, yet staying cool and contained. This was not like fighting. What war asked of you was quite different. What the Isle asked... Only the gods knew.

Presently Clirando, who had not yet drunk, took some wine in a bowl along the shingle and poured out a proper measure for the goddess who seemed to be Maut, Haunter of Waters.

"Let all go well for them, Lady. Protect them and allow them to win honour. For myself, I won't ask you. Nor for sleep. I know, even if you'd grant it, I'd be unable to receive your gift."

Firelight made the zircon eyes sparkle—but only the firelight.

When she went back, they were saying that games were celebrated at a town on the island, deep in its interior, to mark the Seven Nights, and a great fair was held as well, full of wonders, with goods and animals on show that came from remote lands. She wondered where they had heard this. All Clirando had ever heard of the Isle, even on the galley, had been mysterious, uncanny and troubling.

Someone yawned—Vlis.

Clirando said, "I'll take the watch."

"Yes, Clirando." They nodded solemnly. They believed that their leader had trained herself to need little if any sleep on duty. None of them, even Tuy, knew Clirando now seldom slept at all. Why worry them? They boasted of her talent for wakefulness.

As they settled down, Clirando again went off a short way. She sat on a boulder jutting from the stones and sand, about forty paces along the beach. From here she could see all the long curve of the shingle and, beside it, a cliff path that slipped suddenly up along the rock face. It looked to be rough going, but they would use it in the morning.

Would they find other people here quickly? The beacon-lighters perhaps, if no one else.

The sea sighed and crinkled to and fro, lit by phosphorescent runners of foam. Like a lullaby – for some.

In the red circle of firelight, the others had curled up. Already they were all sleeping, heads on rolled cloaks, long legs and folded arms relaxed as the limbs of sleeping cats. Only Tuyamel softly snored, just audible in the quiet. But Clirando was aware the snoring would stop once Tuy was properly asleep.

How well I know them.

I know them better than I know myself.

Clirando regarded the act of sleep. Sometimes it had seemed to her, wandering up to the roof of her own house, she had seen all Amnos sleeping, all the world, with only she herself awake forever.

A pebble, loosened by something or nothing and tumbling down the cliff side, jolted her into a tremendous jump.

Clirando started to her feet, dazzled and alarmed. What had happened? She had *slept—she had slept*? For how long? Her trained eye scanned the stars. From their positions she worked out that all of an hour must have passed.

She did not sleep. She had been watching for hours, now and then prowling up and down along the edge of the sea... and then.

A deadly chill washed through her, and slowly she

turned her head. The campfire burned low, and in its smoky glare she saw that no one now lay curled about it. Every one of her band had vanished.

Clirando ran forward. She kicked the fire up in a blaze, drew out a flaming stick and held it high. Where had they gone – and *why* – without waking her?

All around, the rolled cloaks, undisturbed, the impressions of sleeping heads still pillowed into them. The last baked apples sat along the fire's rim. Nothing else was there, apart from a bit of wood Seleti had been carving, and the wineskin.

Clirando drew her sword. If some enemy were about, he, she or it must be confronted. It was too late for subterfuge.

"Here!" she called.

And then she gave the ululating battle cry of the band. It echoed wildly off the cliffs.

She hoped against hope for some answering call. When her own yell died, none came. Nothing did. Only the sigh of the waves and the thick glimmering sound of the silence.

She could not help herself; a kind of terror was in her. She who could not sleep had slept, and her brave girls – none of them a weakling and all six together – had been taken – or had gone – away.

A weird gleam shone out across the water now. For a moment she could not think what it was. But it was the dawn beginning.

Clirando walked to the sea and plunged in her hands and her feet. The water was night-cold, shocking her back to some sanity.

She was alone, as all were when it came down to it.

She must rely on herself.

Whatever had lured or forced her girls away, Clirando would find it and them.

While the light strengthened in the east. Clirando gathered her few belongings together. As the last stars winked out, she was already on the tortuous path that wound upward from the beach to the high places above.

Just as predicted, it was hard going. When she at last broke out of the thin clinging shrubs onto the plateau of the cliff top, the sun was two hands' width above the sea. Behind and below her the beach and the water. But ahead – Clirando looked inland.

Shoulders and walls of rock palisaded the headland, grey and white and grown with sea ivies and wild peculiar flowers. Quite some way off, the plateau tipped over and down into what seemed to be thick forest of pine and larch, the dark evergreen trees sacred to night and the gods of hidden things. Far in the distance, other heights rose from the forest and stood on the sky.

Nearby a narrow stream of clear water emerged from the natural stonework. Thankfully Clirando drank from it, cupping the water in her hands. It was sour and salty here, too near the sea, but it quenched her thirst.

When she raised her head, a creature was there among the rocks, staring at her. The wildflowers framed it oddly. It was a kind of lion or large lynx, yellow eyed, with a dappled creamy hide.

Clirando pulled the knife free of her belt. She had

hunted where she had to, for food or protection. Though she had never seen an animal quite like this one, she could deal with it if necessary.

The beast fixed its eyes. Against the lean flanks a long tail lashed.

Generally, they did not meet your gaze this long.

Was it magical?

Clirando said, very low, "What do you want?"

The lion creature flung up its head, eyes narrowed and jaws open to reveal lines of white fangs. This gave the irresistibly unsettling impression it laughed. Then, with a final lash of its tail, it sprang around and bounded away between the stands of rock. It had been a male, and obviously not hungry.

Clirando walked toward the plateau's dip and the forest.

By day, the Isle was not so silent. From the shore the cries of seabirds sometimes lifted, and from the forest occasionally other notes. However, these sounds were sparse and intermittent.

For this reason, the faint shuffling and skittering that started to accompany her progress, and which had nothing to do with her own light footfalls, seemed at first an illusion, some obtuse echo stirred up from the aisles of rock as she moved. But in the end Clirando knew her instinct that something followed her must be addressed.

She turned slightly, still going forward – and caught a flash of vague darkness darting behind a rock.

Paying no apparent heed, Clirando strode on, but again she drew her knife.

She could not be sure what tracked her. She did not think it was human. Yet she had not seen enough to judge what sort of animal it might be.

By then she had reached an area where the cliff plateau bulked upward to a stone hill, on the top of which was built one of the great beacons. Unlike the others along the outer coast, this had not been set alight, though a thin smell of old fires clung here. The beacon itself, she saw, was built as a round cauldron of stones, the kindling stacked ready inside and covered by oiled skins, pegged into sockets in the hill. This emblem of human activity both gladdened and disconcerted her.

As she was looking up, the skittery soft scuffle came again at her back, definitely not an echo of her own movements.

Clirando spun round.

She froze.

Three things poised on the rock in a curious huddle – almost as if they were chained together by some invisible rope. They were unlike anything she had ever seen – yet mostly piggish in shape, large pigs covered in an ashy black skin, from which stuck out spines like those of some Lybirican cactus. Their heads were misshapen, with tusks or horns pointing from their jaws, the sides of their faces, and above their small, flat, greenish eyes. Horrible things. Monsters. The very stuff of the legends of Moon Isle.

They made no move to attack.

Clirando took half a step toward them – they neither ran at her nor backed away.

Stooping swiftly, she plucked up a handful of loose

stones and hurled them at the creatures.

They shied a little at the impact, tossing their ugly heads. That was all.

Were they the beasts of some local god?

Abruptly all three peeled back their upper lips. Unlike the lion beast earlier, their teeth were blunt and yellow, but even so not an encouraging sight.

Clirando rasped her sword out of its sheath. She would not turn her back on these things again, she thought.

Exactly then a voice called down from the beacon above.

"Who is there?"

It was the voice of a woman, and not young.

"Stay where you are, Mother," Clirando shouted, "till I deal with these pigs."

The old voice broke into a cackle of laughter. "Pigs? Is that what you see? Deal with them? I doubt you can."

Something came slithering and bouncing down the stone hill behind Clirando.

She turned, affronted but not amazed to be attacked from both sides, and saw a large wedge of dark wet bread falling. It shot past her, landing between her and the pig things.

"Let them have that, whatever they are, a morsel of comfort," called the old woman from the beacon. "And you come up here to me."

Clirando could see the pigs were sniffing after the bread, creeping forward to it, more interested apparently in that than in the warrior girl.

So Clirando jumped at the hill and ran up it, leaping

over the loose stones and tufts of lichen.

At the top she looked back down. The pig things were eating the bread, sharing it in an unusually well-mannered way among them. It had been soaked in wine or beer, and obviously pleased them. One animal raised its head, and from its snout came the strangest sound, a kind of jeering whine – nearly human.

"So, it's pigs, is it?" said the old woman.

Clirando turned again and saw her. She was sitting around the far side of the beacon, weaving on a little upright frame, a cloth of grey and red. "Pigs for you," she said.

"What are they?" Clirando asked.

"Yours," said the woman.

Clirando let out a bark of mirth. "They're nothing to do with me."

"Oh, you think not?"

The woman herself wore a mantle that was grey and bordered by red. She looked ancient as the rock, but her eyes were still black and bright.

"Mother," said Clirando, "thanks for your help. Now perhaps you'll tell me, did a band of girls come by this way, warrior women of Amnos going to the festival of the Seven Nights?"

"Warriors?" asked the old woman. Clirando thought she had a clever, wicked face. "They'd be all in their fighting garb, with swords and such, walking proud?"

Clirando nodded.

"Nothing like that," said the old one.

"Then – Mother – if they went by you, how were they?"

"Oh, I saw no one," said the woman. "I was asleep. I

lie up in that hut over there, while I tend the beacon. Tonight, I must light it for the moon. Fire, to tempt the moon to shine full."

I'll get nothing helpful from her, thought Clirando. The old one had the look she had seen on the faces of certain grannies in the town, who found everything the young did funny, enjoying scorning and misleading them.

"Well, my thanks in any case."

Clirando moved off over the hill. She passed the leaning hut – it looked as if no one had stayed there for ten years or more. Glancing over her shoulder, she noted the old woman had disappeared around a jut of rock. Had she been real?

This is a place of demons and shadows.

At least the pigs were not now on her track. Clirando reached the beacon hill's foot and broke into a fast lope.

She came to the descent and the edge of the forest just before noon. Picking her way down, she found a trail, now and then carved to earthen steps at the steeper spots.

An altar stood by the path side, just in under the trees. A black formless stone was there, with a wooden cup in front of it, holding dregs of honey, from the smell.

Prudently Clirando took out a sweet wafer from her food store and dropped it into the cup.

"I don't know you, but I respect you," she said, bowing to the altar and the stone. Then she went down into the depths of the forest, dark green at noon as the heart of a malachite.

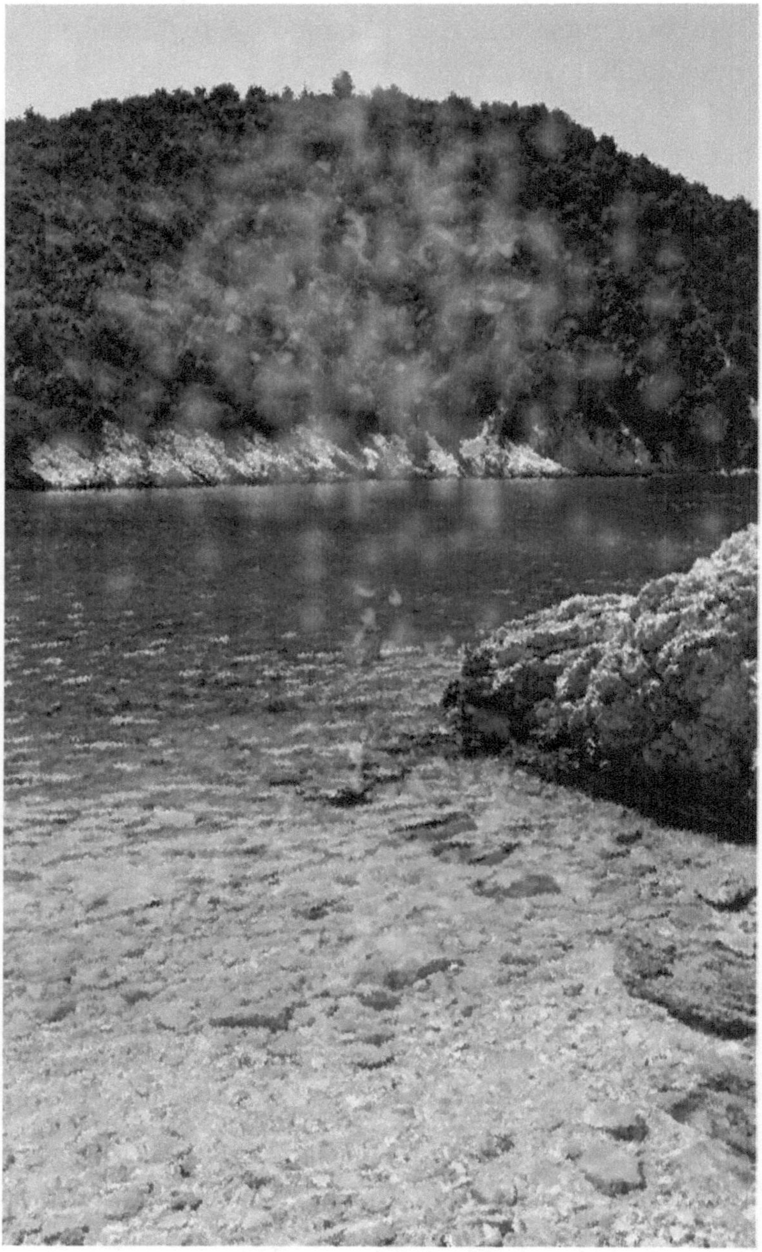

2.

STORY

The pig creatures came back that night, with the dusk.

She had thought she was free of them.

All day Clirando had trekked through the forest. It was dark as a cellar in parts. In others long aisles opened, lit by filtered sunlight. Here and there the conifers gave way to oaks, and even beeches, about whose roots drifts of flowers sometimes lay. But the flowers were small and pale, and the leafy cloudbursts of the canopy seemed full of cores of blackness. In areas the trunks of the pines massed thick as an army, closing off not only all light, but any view or path.

Now and then Clirando heard birdsong. Once – only once – a single grey pigeon sped across from tree to tree. She saw tracks of deer and foxes, once of a wolf, and twice of boar – but none of the animals were ever to be seen. Elusive as the wildlife, her comrades from the band.

Nowhere did she detect any evidence of their passing, either freely or as captives.

Little streams went through the forest, often falling down over tall rocks into some pool below.

By such a pool she decided to make her camp that night and arranged it in the sunset hour.

Clirando took from her pack a handful of oat flour and mixed it with water and raisins, putting the cake to bake in the fire. She sat with her back to the rock, the waterfall splashing softly to her left.

Long shadows gathered as the peachy glimpses of the sky cooled.

Well. There was no fear she would sleep again tonight. Clirando had considered what had happened on the beach. Since she only slept now if drugged, then she *had* been, and her band with her. They had talked quite a while over the food, so probably that was not at fault. Very likely the wine they had brought was the culprit. Clirando, who drank it the last, slept the last. She had left the skin today on the shore, because it was too cumbersome to carry. But who had done it? Who had put the sleeping draft into the wine, and why? Some new enemy?

Tonight was the First Night of Full Moon.

The old woman would be lighting her beacon, and all the other beacons would also beam out again along the coasts. And somewhere the island celebrated like the rest of the world – but where?

Here in these trees she would see the moon, threading through the boughs, clear at the centre of the glade, and over there in that gap.

Clirando ate her oat bread and drank water from the pool. She tried not to think of pirates stealing up the beach to take her drugged girls for slaves. After all, there had been no marks of them anywhere inland. It seemed but too likely now they had been stolen away by ship. Why then did the robbers leave Clirando? Not tempting enough, perhaps, she thought ironically. Thestus had praised her looks, comparing her to a young lion. But Araitha was the beautiful one. And besides Clirando was 'cold' and had no feminine talents…

In a sudden rage Clirando hurled the husk of her bread into the fire. A splash of flame rose there.

"I am not *cold*. I have passion. I showed you that, Thestus, but best I showed you when I beat you in the war-court."

Her voice rang hard on the silence, as if it hit the darkening sky.

And in that moment, from out of the noiseless forest, where not even the birds had sung a farewell to the sun, surged up a piercing, wailing, jeering cry.

Clirando was on her feet, weapons ready.

But after the jeer, silence.

The forest breathed as the sea did, leaves touched by faint night breezes. Not a bird or animal had reacted to the unnerving noise.

She had the rock behind her, the fire and the pool in front. A reasonable defensive position. She waited, tense as the sword in her hand.

Minutes went by, three or four, maybe longer.

Nothing stirred beyond the pool among the columns of the pines.

The cry – some night bird, perhaps, some animal hunting? No, she had never heard such a screech from any animal or bird – or been told of one. But then again, Moon Isle was—

Scalding her ears and brain, searing her heart and blood, the awful wail went up again. *Now* it had three voices.

Human – it was like the jeering of some insane and evil crowd.

She saw them trot, the three of them, from among the trees and the folding cloak of night. The pig monsters from the cliff top.

Clirando bent and drew from her fire a long branch ripe with flames. She held it aloft in her left hand.

Then purposely she walked by the fire, skirting the pool, taking measured steps.

They stood together in a looser formation than before. The beast in the middle lifted its lip, and out came the mocking cry, full blast.

She would move slowly, then sprint straight at them. Fire for the one most to the left, the sword through the neck of the middle one. Then around to take the third with whatever she had.

She was shaking inside herself, but also lit with fury.

What happened then seemed like the childish joke of some cruel god.

Something *else,* rushing like a whirlwind, bowled directly into Clirando, sending her headlong and sprawling. It leaped over her back as she went down – she felt it go, hot as fire.

Pushing herself up, the burning branch lost, the sword juggled back into her grip, she checked in astonishment.

What had knocked her down was the other animal she had met on the cliffs, the lion with the dappled pelt. Either that, or one exactly of the same species. It had jumped over her and gone plunging at the three pig things, just as she had planned to do. As she stood there gasping, she saw how it plummeted straight into all three, angling its leonine body as it did so, the large paws thrashing.

Squealing now, all three pigs jumbled away from it. They went galloping back among the trees, the cat in hot pursuit.

The last she saw of the incredible scene was the lion's creamy tail lashing in darkness like a snake. Then everything was as it had been, and silent once more.

Clirando retrieved the burning branch from the ground and stamped out the scorches it had made. Uneasily, confused, she turned to retrace her way to her fire.

Something else was there.

The reflection of it, fire limned, went down into the pool.

Clirando straightened and raised her sword. Her green eyes were wide and burning like the flames.

"That is my place. Come away from it."

"But you left your place," he said casually.

"Did you see why?"

"I saw something running off through the wood."

Clirando said, "Move over there, away from my fire. I shan't ask you again."

"Were you *asking*? Very well, then. As you like."

When he moved along the poolside and out onto the apron of turf, she never took her eyes from him. He too was a fighter – she could tell from the way he stalked forward, the coordination of his movements. But he had a beauty not often seen among mortal things, found more commonly in well-made statues of young male gods. His hair was so fair it seemed white as mountain snow. White as the moon.

This one also is some illusion or demon.

He stood now about twelve paces from her. Backlit

by the fire, she could see a thin scar high on his right cheekbone, and how the muscles flexed in his arms as he slid the knife he had held back into its sheath. There were darns and recent tears in his clothing, and on one of his boots the silvery trail of a tiny snail that still slid along there, then descended to the grass.

If a facsimile, he was a good one. He looked real.

"We don't have to quarrel, do we?" he inquired pleasantly. "We can share provisions, perhaps. I have some bread and cheese and a little alcohol."

"Who are you? What are you doing here?"

"My name is Zemetrios – Zemetrios of Rhoia. I was told to come here. You too I imagine. Unless this sacred and terrible place is your home."

The sword weighed heavy on her hand. She thrust it back into the sheath, almost startling herself. Tiredness droned in her head and up her spine.

"Very well. I accept your words."

"Then I may share your fire?"

"If you like. It's the oldest law of the gods, isn't it? To welcome the stranger."

"But how unconvinced you sound," he said.

He waited for her to seat herself, but she waved him down first. They sat at opposite sides. Around them the night was now noiseless and, beyond the range of the light, impenetrable.

"The moon will rise in about two hours," he said. He set out his provisions, the cheese and loaf, the flask. Clirando had eaten, but since she had accepted the terms of hospitality, she created another of the oatcakes and handed him an apple. She waited until he had swallowed a bit of the cheese before she would try it.

She saw he noted this, but he said nothing.

She wished he was not here.

They did not speak beyond the barest civilities. After he had drunk from the flask, he offered it to her, having first wiped the lip of the vessel.

Clirando took one sip, for politeness. It was some raw spirit of Rhoia, not really to her taste.

"Since we're two now," he said, "perhaps we should set a watch."

"You speak like a soldier," she said.

"I am – I was. I've fought in the king's legions. Travelled quite a distance, seen the wonders of the world. But that's done now."

His eyes, a clear deep blue, looked away into his past. Clirando could see he beheld something there, bleak and unforgiving.

What else? This place was for testing and penance. For punishment, probably.

She wondered what he had done, then chided herself for being at all interested. He might be dangerous, that was enough to know.

"Well," she said, "I'll take the whole watch. I've already slept my fill." The lie was practiced, ready.

He lifted an eyebrow at her. "You don't trust me, then."

Clirando smiled. "Of course not. Why should I? But I'll take the watch anyway. If anything occurs, I will wake you."

"Wake me when the moon rises," he said. "I want to see it. The last time I saw the Seven Nights I was only eight."

He stretched out with no pretence or air of feeling

vulnerable. His movements were both masculine and graceful, a pleasure for anyone to observe, she thought sourly; a pity they should be wasted on her. "I wonder how it is," he murmured, "she can renew herself these seven times together. Scholars have written," he added dreamily, "there's more than one moon involved in these nights – our own, and six of her sisters she calls from other spheres...." He turned his head a little and fell, apparently, instantly into sleep.

It might be an act. But Clirando thought not. The gods knew, she had in recent months had endless opportunities to study the sleep of others.

And for a stupid instant she felt jealous of his ability to sleep so simply. To her, now, it was an alien concept.

When the moon rose, he woke anyway, the way in fact Clirando herself had often done, sleeping in the open. They said, if the full moon touched your face with her white hand, you roused. In the past of course, Clirando had then gone back to sleep.

"There she is," said the man called Zemetrios. He lay still, looking up.

Together they stared awhile at the bright disk passing over the glade, reflecting like pearl in the pool.

"The moon looks as it always does at full," he remarked.

"What did you expect?"

"Something more – as these are the Seven Nights." He sat up abruptly, stretching, so she heard the strong muscles crack in his arms. "I'll take the watch now, if you like."

"No need," she said.

"Come on, girl. You're a trained fighter. You'd know in a split second if I was trying anything – doubtless you'd kill me."

"Doubtless I would. But I have no difficulty in keeping the watch myself."

He said, "You look tired to your bones."

Clirando blinked, affronted and defensive. "That's for me to judge."

"Then I'll say no more. But at least, will you tell me your name? You have mine."

It was true, in courtesy she owed him that. "Clirando, one of the warrior women of Amnos," she said shortly.

"Yes, I thought you'd be from there. Your bands are highly spoken of." He paused, looking now down into the moon-shining pool. "Clirando, in fairness, I'd like to tell you something of myself. Of what sent me here."

"I ask to know nothing."

"Or you'd *prefer* to stay ignorant of me? Well and good, but this island is no place for human secrecy or deception. Nor do I think it the best place to travel alone."

Scornfully she said to him, her heart beating too fast, "So you're afraid of the Isle? My regrets. But I'm no companion for you. I have my band to think of..." And broke off, aware that she had lost her band and very likely would never find them again. A wide grief swept through her and a sense of shame. She had failed her girls.

He said, "Do me the kindness, then, Clirando, of letting me tell you of my crime. In the temples of the Father, anyone may go and tell his worst sins to a priest, if the burden becomes too great. And I know, in

Amnos, there is also a priestess tradition among the female warriors."

Clirando lifted her eyes from her own emotions and looked at him levelly.

He took this as his cue. Clirando did not know if she had meant it to be one.

"I killed a man," Zemetrios said woodenly. He began to gaze again into the pool. "Fair and square, you might say, in a duel outside my father's house. Or my house, since my father died last year."

Clirando watched him.

The moon lighted his face, but his eyes were shadowed, looking down at the water.

Zemetrios of Rhoia told her how the man he had slain had been his best friend. "We'd fought as comrades in the legions since both of us were seventeen. He was a fine soldier, loyal and trustworthy and clever. We were like brothers from the first. We've fought side by side in enough battles... been promoted to the rank of leader at the same time. I was at his wedding. A pretty girl, a sweet girl. I don't know where she's gone now. She ran away from him, you see. That was after he changed into another man."

A silence.

"What do you mean?" Clirando heard her voice. It had a sound of awe. Zemetrios had caught her with his storytelling. She must be on guard.

Zemetrios said, "He turned into a drunkard. Oh, there had been times in the past – you fight hard, you take leave and drink hard. But those sessions are occasional. Then, with Yazon, they became habitual."

Zemetrios spoke briefly, in terse sentences, of drunk

brawls, meaningless and savage fights with citizens of the town that Yazon, deranged with wine, would pick. "He was a trained fighter. You see what that would mean. They hadn't a chance. He broke their legs and arms and knocked them senseless like cold stones. I and others dragged him off, doused him in the horse trough. Sometimes we would have to chain him up like a mad dog till he sobered."

Yazon began to beat his young wife also. She fled to her parents' house on the hills, and later, after Yazon pursued her there, firstly with gifts, then with threats, to some other land.

"They cast him out of the legions in dishonour. He had only his soldier's pension then, much reduced since he was young and had ruined his own career."

Yazon, Zemetrios said, went to live in an old fisherman's hut near the quay. He begged for his living or committed acts of robbery – twice ending in the jail-pit for a public whipping. All he could get in money went on wine – bad wine, now, the dross of the waterfront taverns.

"I tried my best to help him, Clirando. I'd paid off his debts three times. I'd begged the legion to give him a second chance – twice I did that, but the second time a second chance was refused. He didn't know me mostly anyway, said he thought me some enemy. By then he was never sober. My father was sick by then, too. I had other difficulties, and soon enough the duties of burial and mourning."

Zemetrios paused again.

Clirando said nothing. The tale disturbed her. She empathised with this unknown man and, not daring to trust him – Thestus had won her trust, and Araitha had always *had* her trust – would not speak.

In the end Zemetrios told her that he came from the house one morning to find Yazon lying across the threshold. "He was filthy, covered in sores and fleas, half-dead. I took him in. He had been my friend. What else could I do?"

Cleaned up, fed, and doctored by a physician, Yazon was surly and irritable. Refused more than three cups of wine, he stole it from the cellars, and broke the pitchers in the courtyard when he was done. On a morning when Zemetrios needed to report to the town fort, Yazon attacked two of the kitchen girls. He raped one, and beat them both with a stick, and when someone came running to the fort, Zemetrios raced to his house and pulled the yowling drunkard out into the square. Before a crowd of citizens and soldiers, Zemetrios punched his former friend to the ground, threw him a sword and told him to get up and fight.

"It lasted less than the tenth of an hour. I never meant to kill him – or believed not. But he was no longer Yazon and I perhaps was no longer much myself, either. I'd seen the girls crying. My father had kept a kind and worthy house. The sword pierced him through cleanly enough. He fell over and was dead. Yazon. Dead. I remember," said Zemetrios, "one time in the deserts, marching east, he and I sat looking at the stars and talked about what we wished for ourselves. Both of us wanted only good things. Nothing to anger the gods. But he died on the street and I left my legion and sold my father's house. And now the priests have sent me here."

Clirando had been holding her breath. She let it go carefully, so he should not hear her sigh.

The full moon reached the perimeter of the trees. It slipped behind the canopy, looking for a moment broken in silver pieces, before darkness closed the view.

In the morning Clirando forced herself to alertness. This now was her fifth night without sleep – aside from the deadly drugged hour on the beach. She had not taken much of the herbal medicine on the galley, not wanting her band to guess her predicament, or herself to be unready for any demand the voyage might make. On Moon Isle, she had always realised, she could not risk it at all. Parna's temple had supplied instead a cordial to help her keep her energy and a clear mind. Clirando drank from the vial.

Zemetrios, after he had made his 'confession' to her, had lain back and slept again, but not, she then saw, so well. His slumbers were disturbed. She felt a mean amusement at it. But what if this too were some act?

I can never trust him. He may be a liar and felon. Or – he may not be real at all.

Was such a thing possible? Yes. There were demons here, she had encountered them, for what else were the pig things but some type of animal demon? A man demon might also be feasible. And he had appeared by her fire – as if from nowhere.

She thought grimly, *and enough demoniac men already exist in the human world.*

They shared bread and oatcakes for breakfast. They drank water from the pool.

He told her then that the priests in Rhoia had assured him a large village lay at the heart of the Isle, deep in the forest and below the mountains. This was where the Seven Nights were celebrated. "We should make for there."

Was this a lie, too? Or a trap?

But she could think of nothing else to do. Against all common sense she had a wild hope the girls of her band might be at this village, part of the celebration they themselves had discussed.

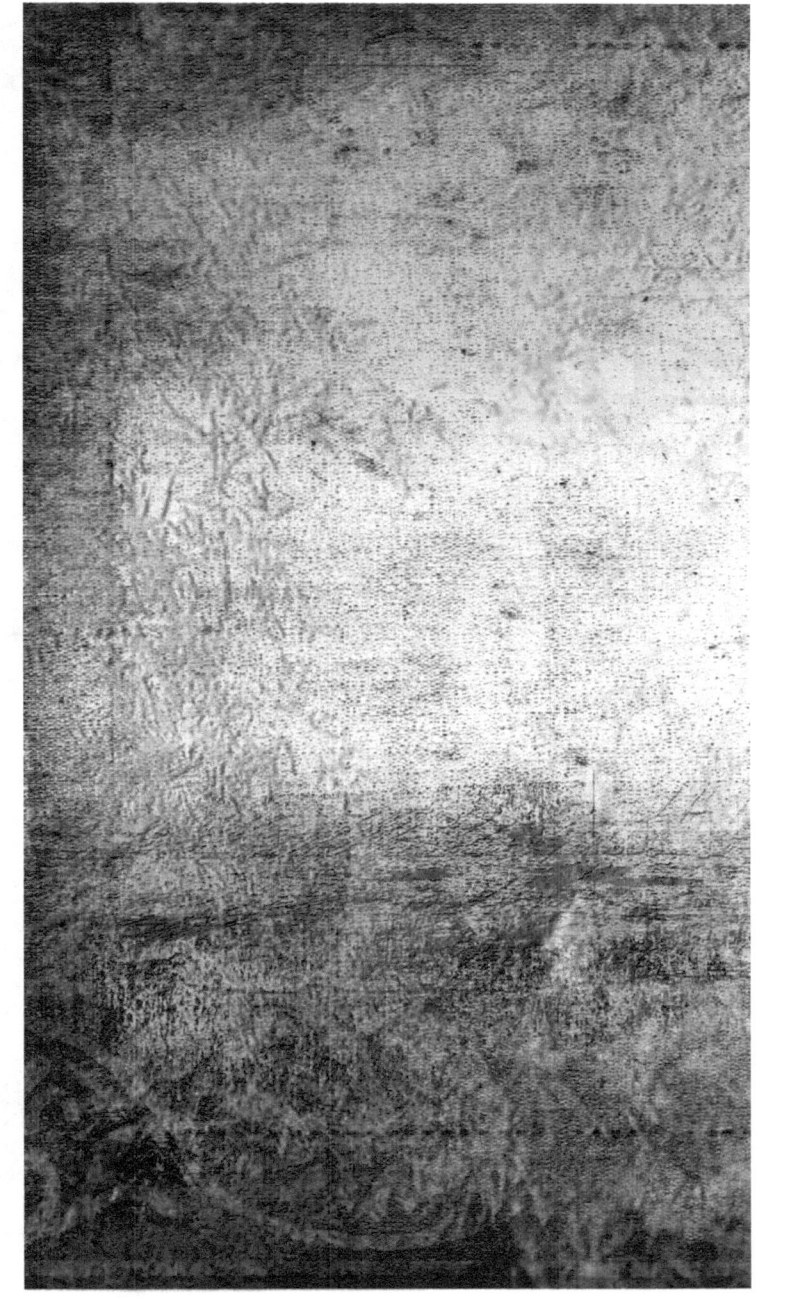

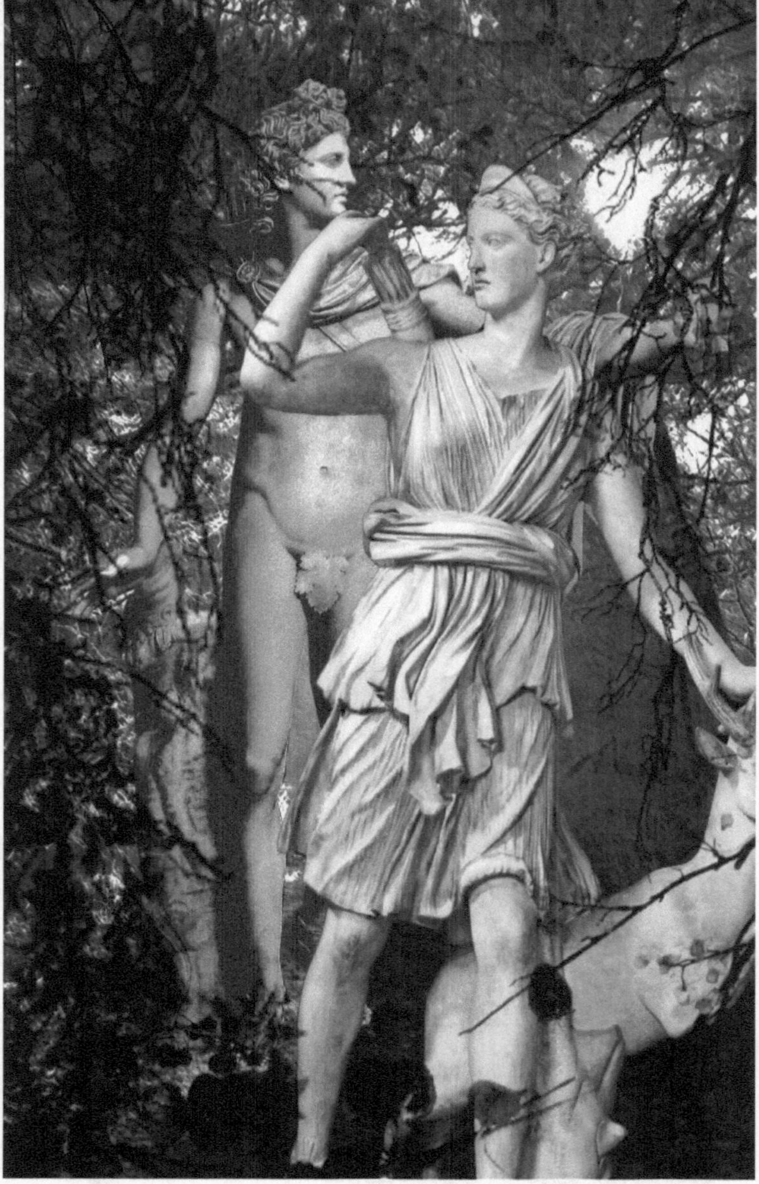

3.

JOURNEY

They both moved at a steady lope along the continuing track that ran through the trees. Everything was as it had been, a hot day burning up behind the leaves and pine needles, freckled sun-shafts, cool shadows, little wayside streams, rocks, and the rare sound or sight of a bird, and once a yellowish fox trotting over their path.

Near noon they came into another glade, without water, but the turf covered with drifts of the pale flowers. Vines hung from the trees like nets, jewelled by fast-ripening grapes.

They paused here, picking and eating the fruit.

From behind the walls of the pines, there came suddenly a jeering, eerie whoop.

He heard it too, she thought.

Transfixed, Clirando saw a dark huddle of shapes ruffling along behind the curtains of the vines. There were more of them now. A whole pig herd of these demons of hers.

Last night she had yearned that the lion cat would catch and devour them. But obviously, even if it had, other members of the tribe existed.

"What is it?" Zemetrios said to her.

They had, until then, spoken very little, and of nothing beyond their own advance, the grapes, and the mooted village.

Shaken again, Clirando said, "Animals."

He stared over where she did. "Or," he said, "supernatural things."

"Can you see them?" The question burst from her before she could decide to withhold it.

"Something... but the island is full of such stuff. They trouble you?" he asked, turning his blue eyes full on her.

Angrily Clirando said, "What business is it of yours?"

"Only this – I too am tormented by creatures or images that roam through the trees. Not animal in that sense. They call to me in drunken voices... insubstantial. An army of drunken ghosts."

As he said this, clear as if drawn in paint, Clirando saw Araitha standing between two pines. She wore her traveller's cloak, and her golden hair with its ornaments caught the sunlight. Her face had no expression.

Clirando began to tremble. She told herself dizzily that it was only her sleepless eyes that played the trick.

She shut them, which was a mistake, and felt Zemetrios catch hold of her, lifting her clear of some abyss into which she had been about to fall.

She pushed him away. His strength and quickness alarmed her. She was humiliated by her own weakness.

But he would not let her push him off. He held her up and put the flask against her mouth.

"Take some."

"No."

"It's only water. I drank the last of the spirits last night."

Clirando drank. The water was still cold, and despite his words, kept the tang of alcohol. It steadied her.

"My thanks. Let go of me now. I'm well."

"You're not. But yes, I'll let go. There."

She could smell him, the health of his young body, the clean aroma of his hair and breath.

Clirando glanced at the pines.

The ghost was gone.

"Did you kill her?" Zemetrios asked.

"*What*?"

"You spoke a name, two in fact. A man's name and a woman's. You spoke *his* name with utter scorn. And hers with – forgive me, warrior girl – with *fear*."

Clirando dropped herself down to her knees and sat back. She no longer felt faint, but drained and – what Araitha had promised – *empty*.

This man *was* real. She had disgraced herself by nearly fainting in front of him like some pampered lady. What did the truth matter now?

"I killed her. Not directly. But she died because of what I did."

"Because she lay down with your lover? Oh, Clirando, it isn't hard to guess. You spoke two names, remember?"

"She lay down with my lover. She'd been my friend. Him I beat in fair fight and he was sent away. She also. She went to Crentis, but the ship sank. She's dead, as you say. Through me."

"By the Father," said Zemetrios softly.

"She cursed me, too." Clirando gave a small rasp of laughter. "I can't sleep. A slight curse, you might think."

"No, I don't think that."

"Well," said Clirando, "let's get on."

She stood up again.

The forest was silent and black beyond the sunlight of the vine glade. Like all her life surely now, beyond that night when lightning struck Parna's Temple.

Why did I trust him? Stupid, to blab it all out to him. Are you a child, or what? Well. He knows now.

Clirando ran lightly beside Zemetrios, through the glints and shades, angry with herself, lamenting, full of pain.

Nothing had importance, only to go on, to find her band. Or if not, respectfully to complete this awful and weird penance set her by the priestesses of the Maiden. And then be done with all of it.

I too will go away. Into the East perhaps, where people lose themselves. Because already I'm lost. Who is Clirando? Clirando would never have blurted out her secret to some stranger.

But as they loped shoulder to shoulder, glancing up at the 'stranger', from time to time she saw the twitch behind his eyes, and once his head turning, then snapping around again. He too heard and saw devils in the forest as he had said, that fact alone was certain.

And she – she came to hear sometimes an unearthly low sound that filtered through the trees like wind, though the leaves never moved. It had for her no noise of drunken voices – the multiplied voice of Yazon in all the moods of his insanity. If she detected anything it was the jeering cry of the pig things – but now never too close.

Possibly he had been right. To travel together might provide a little distance for both of them from their haunts. Even the ghost of Araitha had not drawn near.

Had it been she? For sure?

Clirando frowned as she ran. *They are my devils. They come for me. Out of my heart and mind. It's only that the forest makes them real. But how real? Could I have gone to her and seized her, run her through with a knife?*

Clouds massed across Clirando's eyes. She half stumbled, and he turned and looked at her. His face was concerned, curious.

"A root," she said.

And pushed memory and idle surmise to the edges of her brain.

The trees began to thin out near sunfall.

The downward slopes were more gradual, and oak trees and wild olive predominated. Here the track ended abruptly. Another altar place stood there, this one with a whitish stone roughly carved and pocked, a sort of uneven globe.

He and she halted beside it. In the bronzy light now slanting sidelong through the trees, the globe seemed to pulse with uncanny inner light.

Clirando took the last honey wafer from her pack and laid it by the stone. "I do not know you, but I reverence you."

Zemetrios, rather sheepishly, she thought, put the final sliver of cheese on the altar. It was mostly rind. Any god would disdain it – or perhaps not, since they would otherwise have eaten it.

"Look," he said quietly.

A hare bounded among the olives, its long ears brushed with light and glowing red.

They could have brought the hare down for supper, either of them, she was certain. But in this place neither had wished to, or though it wise.

Did they in some ways, then, think alike?

No.

Remember Thestus, the arch deceiver. Though Thestus, she believed, would have wanted to throw his knife or a rock at the hare, and she would have had to stop him.

As they turned from the altar, Clirando saw an old man sitting about fifty paces away under a broad-leaved tree. His hands were busy with something that sparkled – and she was positive he had not been there in the preceding moments.

"Do you see him?"

"Yes," Zemetrios said.

Slowly they walked forward, making no attempt at caution. The old man did not look up. But when they were almost within arm's length of him, he raised his aged face. His eyes were black and keen in the pleated paper of his skin.

"You're going to the village," he told them, "the Moon Town."

"It exists, then," said Clirando.

"Perhaps," said the old man.

What spangled through his hands was a threaded skein of brilliant stones – like Eastern rubies and diamonds they looked. He seemed only to be playing with them and suddenly he cast them down.

Zemetrios but not Clirando sucked in breath.

Meeting the ground, the sparkly web changed instantly to a long and coiling snake, marked along its back with points of red and silver.

"Oh," said the old man, sarcastically polite, "did I make you jump, bold soldier?"

"Yes, Father," said Zemetrios. Good-naturedly he laughed. "You're a magician, then."

"Sometimes a magician. Sometimes other things. Sometimes I am a tree."

They regarded him wordlessly. The burnished snake poured itself away and up the narrow trunk of a nearby olive.

"Things come, and also they go," said the old man.

"How great a distance to the village now, Father?"

"Not far. Be there before sunset ends. They close the gates at first dark."

"A wise precaution," said Clirando.

She guessed Zemetrios, as she did, tried to draw the old man out, provoke him into some revealing word or action.

But he did not reply now, only took from the inner folds of his garments another skein of beads. Moving it to and fro between gnarled hands, he crooned what must have been the spell to make a serpent out of it.

"Well, good evening to you," said Zemetrios.

He and Clirando walked on.

About twenty steps farther along, both of them turned as one. Only shadows sat under the broad-leaved tree.

"The snake-maker, I shall call him that," said Zemetrios.

"It was a trick, an illusion."

"Maybe. Did you see how he did it?"

"No. But then often you never can – that is the idea of it."

"I met an old woman, too," Zemetrios said, "the first day, when I'd climbed up from the beach. There was an unlit beacon there. She wove only cloth, not snakes. She said she lived in a hut."

"I met her also. The hut hadn't been used for years."

"What are they?" he said softly, as they paced on again. "Are they demons, too? If so, I don't recognise them."

"Not all demons are recognisable."

"You're sensible, Clirando."

She shrugged.

The ground sloped up now. The trees were much fewer in number, long stretches of grass and weeds between them, and no path anywhere, as if, though many walked through the forest, none ever came as far as this.

The sun, which they could see now, hung low in the sky, a red ball in a curdling of gold and scarlet cloud.

They had reached the top of the hill. They looked down into the small basin of a valley.

Impending sunset described it exactly. Fields and groves, vineyards and orchards clustered there. And from them protruded high walls of dressed stone, above which showed tiled roofs, and one tall slim tower. The village. Behind everything, mountains rose, three peaks, one behind another, and touched sidelong with flame by the dying sun.

The way down to the valley was easy. The slope was broken now by another pathway, itself of laid stone, and broad enough for three men to walk together.

"At first dark the gates shut," he repeated.

They broke into a racer's run, leaping down the roadway into the valley.

4.

VILLAGE

Shadows are called
By the ending of the day
Night unfolds her wings
With the white moon in her hair...

Clirando shuddered. The fragment of song had sounded inside her skull, words clear as the plinking of the lyra which accompanied them – so clear, for a moment she thought a voice had actually sung aloud, a hand actually plucked the chords. Araitha's voice and Araitha's hand. It had been a favourite song of hers to play after supper.

Zemetrios this time did not seem to notice Clirando's lapse.

He said, "There are no lights in this village."

Clirando said, "Nor any lights anywhere among the fields and orchards. Not one torch burning. Not a single dog to bark."

The sun was just now down over the horizon, leaving a solitary rift of gold. Darkness was claiming the landscape. But not a lamp shone out anywhere, and over the stubble of the fields, where already the grain must have been scythed, not one figure walked. The orchards too had been stripped of fruit, which surely would not have been ripe.

"What's happened here?" Zemetrios asked.

The walls of the village-town lay ahead of them, and in them two tall wooden gates stood wide. A street of tamped earth ran in from there, and buildings lined the way. But there also – no movement, and no illumination.

"We must go and see," she said.

The thought of her girls was in her mind. They had vanished—and now this deserted village.

They hurried to the gates, and reached them as the final golden wash faded on the sky's edge and darkness bloomed like a long sigh over the earth.

"*Look*! The gates are *closing…*"

Together, not thinking, caught by some primal instinct, they bolted between the slowly joining gates. Clirando cursed herself even as she did so – to pelt into this unknown enclosure that might contain anything – and heard Zemetrios curse louder.

But by then they were in.

The gates padded together at their backs.

And, in a fiery chorus, at once every lamp, torch and candle in the village was, or began to be, lit.

The village street, the houses and other buildings, blushed to sudden life. Faces appeared at windows and figures emerged on terraces. Others came strolling along the thoroughfare. Two men, that neither she nor Zemetrios, she thought, had previously seen, were securing the gates with bars.

"Just in time, travellers," one of the men remarked to them.

Then down the street came striding a giant creature,

tall as the roofs, her black hair swinging as she swung her impossibly long legs, a lighted brand in her grasp with which she brought alive the last torches leaning from house walls.

Zemetrios laughed. Clirando glared at him. Had he gone crazy?

"A stilt-walker, Clirando," he said.

And looking back, Clirando saw the woman, who was dark skinned as a Lybirican, was perched on two long poles, each swathed in her abnormally long white skirt.

A child ran up then. She carried a basket of apples and dates and offered it to them.

Zemetrios reached out at once.

Clirando said, "Be wary."

"I'm hungry, Clirando."

"Yes, but if you eat that you may also be dead."

"Or," he conceded, "this is magic food."

But the child waited there, smiling and holding up the basket, which had been lined with vine leaves.

Before either of them could decide, a man rode by on a brown horse and called the child to him. Bending from the saddle, he took a fruit and bit into it.

"Are these truly people?" Zemetrios asked, "that one there on the horse, the child – or are they another sort of demon – illusions – even figments come from our own heads?"

"We both see the same things here," said Clirando, "men with snakes, lamps lit, a horseman and a child. A basket of fruit."

"Yes. But suppose..."

Another man tapped Zemetrios on the shoulder.

Zemetrios shot around to find the fellow bowing low. He wore the leather apron of tavern staff.

"Come to our inn-house, warriors. It is a fine house. The best wine on the Isle. Good meat and new-baked bread. Our rooms are of the nicest – though we're full for the celebration of the Seven Nights, still one or two choice chambers remain. We also boast a bath house, and water always hot from a steamy spring. Come to our house, warriors."

"He sounds like any tavern tout from Rhoia to Ashalat," murmured Zemetrios.

The man swayed, beaming and bowing.

All through the village circulated the usual evening street sounds, laced now with rills of laughter and notes of music.

Above, a woman called across from one balcony to its neighbour, and in another window another woman appeared with a little pet dog on her shoulder.

The scene was normal. Perplexingly so. As he had said, Rhoia – or anywhere thriving in the civilized world – would parade like this after sundown. Even Amnos.

Clirando said to the taverner, "What's the name of your inn?"

"*The Moon in Glory*."

Zemetrios added, "And why does your village hide until the gates are shut? And why is there no one out in the fields and not a single light?"

"Oh, master, it's our custom on the Seven Nights. Soon as the sun starts to sink, we sit in quiet and not a candle's lit till the last ray's gone. Then we shut the gates and every light is kindled. As for the country about, why – everyone's here. Of course they are. Where else to see and salute the great moon?"

Zemetrios turned to Clirando. "Do we believe him?"

"Oh, *believe* me, master..." The taverner had a round face that now grew anxious. "The innkeeper will be displeased if I lose him custom." Sidling nearer, the man whispered, "He's a skinflint, and he loves to make money."

"Ah, *money*. Then I reckon this is real enough."

Clirando looked about her. Her weariness pushed against her back and shoulders. Who cared if it was a trap or an illusion...? She should not think this way. But she said, "We can see for ourselves."

The man skipped before them up the street and along an alley to a blue-plastered wall, out of which a lemon tree grew, its hard, green fruit scenting the air.

A boy, all smiles as well, whisked open a gate into a yard. Torches blazed on walls; night-perfumed flowers spilled luxuriously from urns. There was additionally the smell of good bread and roasting joints, and over the low wall steam puffed from the domed roof of a little bath house, just as promised.

"Oh, Clirando – forgive me. I can't resist." Zemetrios sounded both amused and charming.

"Nor I," she admitted, but with chilly reserve.

Yet from nowhere the oddest feeling fled through her. What in the Maiden's name was it? In dismay, Clirando accepted it had been a moment's natural pleasure. As if her life was quite natural too, and the town her friend, and Zemetrios, this unknown fighter from another country, someone she trusted, liked, and perhaps much more...

Night unfolds her wings
With the white moon in her hair
And love rises from her bed of dreams
To waken all the sleeping earth.

"What is it, Cliro?"

She gazed at him, stricken. "I can hear a song..."

"I can hear it, too. About night and the moon and love. I've heard it in Rhoia. It's an old tune."

Something loosened in her. She thought, *even if this is fakery, we both see and hear the same things now. Something in that. And besides, that voice singing is a boy's. Not hers – not Araitha's...*

It was only after they had parted to seek the male and female sections of the bath that she recalled Zemetrios had called her *Cliro*. As if long familiar with her, and close.

Despite the taverner's boast, the inn seemed not that full – or certainly not the bath house. Clirando had the three narrow rooms to herself. She washed in the first under the tepid fountain, and then soaked in the second in a pool of delicious heat that blanketed her up to the chin. An attendant in the first room washed her hair. Now it spread about her in the hot pool, scented like the perfumed shrubs outside. Finally, she sprang into the last cold pool, with a hiss of anguish that quickly disappeared as the water toned her muscles, closed her pores and awarded her a feeling of vigour. She might have slept a whole night through. It seemed to her there must be special salts in the spring that fed the bath house, which was often the case. She felt literally renewed, her eyes clear and well-focused, her blood moving like waves of light.

Unnerving her less now, the feeling of pleasure, almost of happiness and anticipation, continued and grew stronger.

She thought of Tuyamel tilting her head doubtfully, and Vlis chuckling, and young Draisis enthusiastically vindicating happiness at all costs.

I'll find them, Clirando thought, kicking her feet in the cold water as a child might. *I shall find them here. This village, tonight – or tomorrow. I'll ask, and I'll look for them.*

But she knew her exhilaration had to do also with Zemetrios.

She felt lenient with herself. Why should she not be glad at the company of an apparently decent and highly attractive man?

Every reason.

But as that warning voice stirred at the back of her mind, Clirando kicked it up in the air with the sprays of cold water. Then she climbed out and dried herself, shaking her hair like a dog.

He had already commandeered a table for them and two benches, tucked into a wall nook. He had ordered beer, which generally Clirando preferred to wine. She thought he himself did not care that greatly for wine – understandable, if he had seen its ill effect on Yazon.

They talked to each other now freely, again as if well-known to each other and quite at ease. But the subjects of the conversation were only the excellence of the hot water, the types of food the inn offered. All around, a crowd massed at the tables, and serving girls and men went to and fro. Clirando saw no one else she knew.

"I have hopes my band of girls reached this village," she said at last. "I was separated from them after we brought in the boat."

He looked at her, consideringly. It was like a question, and reluctantly, after a few seconds, she heard herself say, "They vanished from the beach. They'd been sleeping– and I too – I fell asleep, which now I never can, unaided. There was some drug in the wine."

Before she knew it would happen, he put his hand briefly, and warm, over hers. "I'm sorry, Clirando. I've heard so many tales like that about Moon Isle. It will come right. You'll make it so."

His touch chimed upward through her flesh. She stared resentful at her own hand, as if waiting to see a burn or scald appear where his fingers had rested. Gruffly she said, "I mean to walk about the village, to see if I can learn anything."

"Don't ask any of them here," he said, surprising her. "I'd guess you'll learn nothing that way."

"I thought you believed this inn – this village – trustworthy."

"Did I say that? No. I said it was all irresistible."

She saw he too was looking intently at her hand. Suddenly he said, "I like your hand, Clirando of Amnos. Forgive me, but the firmness, and the callus there from a warrior's knife. My first love, I have to tell you, was a warrior woman. Even before that, my mother had belonged to a band. But then she wed my father and gave it up."

Clirando frowned. "Did he force her to?"

"No. He was an honourable man. It was her choice. She never lost her edge, though. She would wrestle the other girls for practice, and she could ride as well as any man, better than many. She was the one who taught me horses."

The food came, and they ate, dipping the warm bread among the sauces, tearing off chunks of the succulent roast.

Around and about, the inn went on as inns did everywhere in the known world. Clatter of dishes, clink of metal cups, mirth and singing, the occasional quarrel roused and calmed. Abruptly a long, high call went through the room. "The moon! She's risen!"

Not one person kept their seat. Even the servers went out. They all stood on a high open terrace above the yard. There on the wall balanced the moon, round and blazing white.

"Yes," said Zemetrios, "something new after all. She looks whiter here, don't you think? Clean and cold."

A man spoke behind them. "It is the snows that cover her."

Clirando turned.

A merchant, well dressed and well groomed, wiping his ringed, dinner-greasy hands on a napkin.

"Snow?" Zemetrios queried. He smiled.

"Indeed. So our sages tell us. At midsummer in this, our world, up there midwinter comes. The snows fall thickly. And so the moon shines so white."

"The moon is also a world, then?" Clirando asked innocently. It was what the priestess had said. But she thought of Zemetrios's stricture: to ask anything here would be profitless. Perhaps something so esoteric would not matter.

"Do you see that mountain?" The merchant pointed back over the roof of the inn, the other roofs of the village, and up into the sky where all three peaks showed, as if faintly drawn on by a brush. "The central height is known as Moon's Stair. There is, they say, an entrance up there that leads between the worlds and out onto the surface of the moon. Sleepers often travel to the moon, as do sorcerers, or priests in a trance. But physically there's only one way, and that is by climbing the mountain called Moon's Stair."

Zemetrios said, "I've heard of an entrance to the lands beyond death. That's in the East."

"Like that, then," said the merchant. "Or maybe it's all lies." His grin was crafty, knowing. It seemed he understood quite well what Zemetrios had said to Clirando earlier.

Down in the yard, servants were lighting the tails of firecrackers. Now they dived upward on flights of glittering topaz.

Clirando thought, *Surely they would have done this last night, too – we should have heard something of it, seen it even, far above the forest...*

She was unable to feel alarm at this, not even suspicion.

When she glanced back, the merchant had gone in, returning apparently to his meal.

Others were jostling down the terrace steps and across the courtyard.

"Come watch the magicians!" came the cry now.

"Shall we go and see the fun?" he said.

"Perhaps."

"If your girls are here, no doubt they'd go to see. Isn't that the best chance?"

Clirando thought of Draisis and fifteen-year-old Erma. She nodded.

As they followed the rest of the people out of the alley and along one of the wider village streets, Zemetrios said in her ear, "One further thing, Clirando. The inn's so full the taverner could offer us only a single apartment – I mean it has only one bed. He seemed to reckon us partners, but I assured him you would use the room and I would take a place in the common area."

Clirando was jolted. She did not know why, then thought she did. "No, Zemetrios. You take the room. You know I never sleep. A place on a bench is less trouble for me."

"No, Cliro. You must have the bed. It's more comfortable, particularly if sleep eludes you."

"What?" She scowled at him. "You think me some soft little lady? Even when I could sleep, I managed as well on a rock as a couch."

Zemetrios burst out laughing.

For an instant her annoyance increased – then melted. Clirando began to laugh, too. "Excuse me," she said. "Of course you'd think of nothing of the sort."

"Of course not."

"It was only your fairness, offering me the bed. I thank you, but no need. You take it."

Still following the crowd, they were turning now into an open square.

"We'll argue it later," he said.

The moon fired white arrows through the garden

vines that overhung the square. The tall narrow tower, seen previously, rose from one corner, and nearby was a temple to the Father, its crimson-painted columns gilded with torchlight. A grove of trees grew in the centre of the space. They were clearly sacred, carefully shaped conifers, strung with baubles and little masks made from fine Lybirican paper. A line of four men sat cross-legged on the ground before the grove. They wore vivid clothing sewn with glinting beads, red, yellow, green, and blue.

The people elsewhere in the square had also sat down except for latecomers at the back, among whom were Clirando and Zemetrios. Behind them was only the high wall of a house.

To begin with, the four magicians acted out a short play. They were travelling performers, Clirando thought. But during the drama, a burlesque that concerned a runaway servant, a harsh master and a mischievous god, magical effects abounded. At first, they were of the sort that Clirando had watched many times from such troupes at Amnos: birds flying out of sleeves, coins found in ears, objects disappearing and then reappearing somewhere unexpected. Bit by bit, however, the magic became more miraculous, and much stranger. The man in the yellow robe, who played the servant, opened wide his mouth – and out darted a silver frog, swiftly pursued by six other silver frogs from the same spot. All these bounced about the square, finally leaping together and becoming a silver ball, which rolled away under the blue robe of another man, he who played the god. The actor who played the master meanwhile lit a fire on the bare earth by sneezing – or pretending to sneeze – directly at it. The fourth mage-actor, who had taken all the other parts, suddenly assumed the head of an ass. Clirando could not see how he managed this. One moment he was man-headed and the next not. The ass-head was also extremely convincing, waggling its ears and letting out mad brayings through wrinkling lips.

The play ended with the cruel master punished and the servant rich. All four then danced a maniacal stamping dance to the twanging accompaniment of entirely invisible musicians.

Laughter had rumbled through the crowd, shouts of approval, encouragement or chagrin at the plight of the characters. Clirando and Zemetrios were not immune. They had laughed and shouted, too.

The fourth magician now reached into the fire and drew out two handfuls of it.

Flames burned and flickered in both hands, matching his red robe and lighting up his face. Then the fires froze. It happened slowly and completely. *Then* he held up before them two dully glowing bunches of steaming orange ice. These were passed into the audience, which in turn passed them around.

When they had reached the back of the crowd, both Zemetrios and Clirando were able to examine these ice-flames. They certainly were ice-cold, sweating at the warmth of the night – as ice would have done. After she had handed them on to her neighbour, she rubbed her frozen fingers and thought, *these mages are very great.*

Next thing, the magicians pointed up into the sky. Above, the moon was lifting toward the zenith. Only the most engorged stars gleamed strongly enough to be seen against her extravagant light.

The magicians started to wave their arms and call up at the heavens. "Stars! Stars come down and visit us! No one will miss you up there, on such a moon-white night."

And the stars came.

They detached themselves from the black sky, circling, *swarming* like diamond bees down toward the island.

Clirando heard Zemetrios murmur beside her. She too was astounded and filled by the wildest happiness. Why should stars *not* fall from heaven? If they did, what else wonderful might not be able to occur? The laws of the gods were often so harsh. Did this magic signify such laws might be broken?

Scintillant, in drifts, the stars began to festoon the trees. Some were large as a platter, others small as a brooch. They lit up the square with a pure, bluish radiance.

Others fell into the hands of the magicians, who began, carelessly, to juggle with them. Arcs and firebursts dazzled as these tinier orbs dashed from hand to hand.

The show went on, hypnotically, until a far-off note sounded from above, musical as any lyra.

"She calls them back!" the crowd bellowed. "The moon wants her children home again!"

And the mages let go the spangled stars, which swirled together, while others swooped from the trees to join them. A vortex of white fire spun above the square, then flew upward.

The great light faded. Each star must be fitting itself back into its place. Clirando thought she saw several do this, settling in unseen sockets in the velvet dark.

The four mages stepped forward, brushing off their palms—as if the stars had left a slight stellar pollen on them.

What now?

Clirando realised Zemetrios and she stood so close their shoulders and arms were in continual contact. His right arm – sworn arm. Her left. She had not noticed before, as if this were quite natural.

The magicians were reaching out now toward the grove of sacred trees. Also, as if *this* were natural, they were drawing down the boughs, drawing them outward and over. Like tall cloaks of thick black-green fur, the trees unravelled, bringing their baubles and decorative masks with them, and wrapped all four figures round.

The men vanished into the mantle of the trees. Then the trees *smoked*. The whole square of people breathed as the mass of men and conifers coiled and spiralled up into the sky – up to where the stars had gone, and the white mask of the moon.

But where men and trees had been…

A creamy lion prowled the centre of the square beside a patterned lynx with emerald eyes, an antlered deer black as ebony, a tusked elephantus from the East, heavy with long grey hair – which, providing its own fanfare, trumpeted.

The crowd shrieked, applauded, scrambled to its feet in a mixture of fright and pleasure.

"Illusions," Clirando murmured.

"Dreams," said Zemetrios.

But the animals too sprang upward now. Like the rest, they surged away into the air.

Smaller and smaller they became. At the last moment four flashes like miniature lightnings occurred.

Each creature became one last star, just visible against the brilliance of the moon.

"I've heard all men," Zemetrios said, "have a spirit animal that lives inside their soul. Perhaps..."

Perhaps.

Zemetrios escorted Clirando up the inn stair to the allotted room. It lay deep in the house, behind winding corridors and countless other chambers, from most of which eddied quiet voices, and now and then unstifled cries of delight.

The whole village had become flagrantly amorous. Returning from the display in the square, they passed through laughing, kissing groups, couples dancing with linked hands to the music of flutes, their eyes fixed only on each other. By shadowy walls, under courtyard trees, embraces. Arms about each other, mouths fused, lost only in the world of love – two becoming one.

A sadness had stirred in Clirando. She shook it from her. She would not become one of those who grudged other women the joy of lovemaking. After all, Oani and Seleti among her girls had both had lovers.

There had been no sign of the band anywhere. Surely they would have come to see the magicians, as almost all the village had seemed to. She believed she had not taken enough notice of their absence as she should.

If they were not here, then... Then tomorrow she must search.

Let me fret about that, not give in to pointless jealousy.

She kept her mind on the problem as she and Zemetrios walked through the inn to the room they were not to share.

The door was of old wood, carved with a sort of tree, a tree of fruit, but the carving was rough and had faded away, sanded off by time. Even so, it was a splendid room when once they had opened the door. The window had been shuttered though the night remained close and warm. Clirando undid the shutters. Outside, the village curled away into the dark, hardly a light anywhere aside from a few last smouldering torches.

They lit the room's two candles. Despite the low ceiling, the chamber was large, and clean. The bed too was large, heaped with covers and furs as if for the cold months.

He said, "Maybe after all you'll sleep tonight."

She said nothing, knowing she would not.

"I'll look forward to seeing you again, in the morning. Rest well."

"Wait."

"Yes, Cliro?"

Her back to him still, she said crisply, "This is a great cave of a room. Why not stay? There's space for both of us, and enough pillows and covers for an army... enough therefore to spare if one of us sleeps on the floor."

When he did not reply, she turned and looked at him. In the dull light she could not read his face, saw only the slight scar on his cheekbone, the lucent steadiness of his eyes.

"If you trust me," he said.

"I trusted you in the forest," she answered flatly. "Or rather, Zem, I trusted *myself* if you were *not* to be trusted."

I too have now called him by a familiar name – did I mean to?

He lowered his head. It was a meek gesture belied by his tall, muscular frame, and for a second she *did* not trust him. But then he said, "You *can* rely on me, Cliro. Don't insult me by making out I'm a mannerless oaf. I won't lay a finger on you. However much..."

She waited. What had he meant to say? However much he would *like* to?

The excitement of the night still fizzed in her blood like strong-spiced wine. *Be careful!*

She pointed at the bed. "This is a wide couch."

He did not speak.

Clirando drew her sword. "Do you know the custom?"

"Yes. A woman and a man who must sleep in the same bed put a sword between them, and so keep chaste."

"Here's mine, then," she said. "We'll both lie down here. Neither of us is a baby, let alone a dishonourable fool. What do you say?"

Another sword rasped, and candlelight slid down it as it in turn was drawn from his scabbard. He placed it in reverse, head to toe with hers, the hilt under the tip of her blade, her hilt upon his point.

"Agreed."

Either side the bed, looking down at the swords which already lay and slept there, she and he.

"Well," she said.

"Do you prefer I sleep clothed?" he said.

Something flamed at Clirando's centre. No use to deny it. None at all. Nor to deny – she had *not* been careful.

"Only if you prefer. We've pledged faith. Strip if you want. I'll turn my back."

So she turned again, honourably enough.

Behind her she heard the click and rustle of his garments undone and coming off. And – there, on the wall, Clirando saw his shadow reflection, clear in every detail, drawing the tunic over his heard, unbuckling his belt.

Did she dare look around at him?

She wanted to.

Her core was full of fire, leaping and alive – no longer frozen flame, defrosted by desire…

Abruptly, he cursed.

At the signal, irresistibly, Clirando spun about.

"What is it?" she lamely demanded, hardly knowing what she said, her eyes full only of Zemetrios, standing naked before her.

"A sharp bramble from the wood caught in my boot – it had a sting…" he said, explaining the curse, breaking off.

His body was tanned and beautifully made, as it had promised to be. Again she thought of statues of gods, but this one was living. From the width of his shoulders to the narrowness of his hips, the coordination of arms, the long legs – perfect – aside from the scars of old wounds that marked him. Yes, he was soldier and warrior. So much was obvious.

"What caused that scar?"

"This? Oh, that was at Ashalat three years ago. A spear. He lived just long enough to regret it."

"And that one, over your ribs?"

"A knife. I can't recall – Disbuthiem, I think, in the Northern Isles. Or was it Bas Bara?"

"That one, then, on your stomach?"

"Oh, *that* one. My first year as a soldier. My own fault. I managed to stab myself at practice. Shameful." He laughed. His laugh was golden, like his body and his beauty. Unselfconscious – no, flaunting himself, yet in such a still, couth way.

He gave however no sign of wanting her. Judging from evidence already clearly before her, that would have been a proud show, too.

Did she dare go over and touch him – that slender final long-healed wound on his thigh...? Would he recoil?

He did not want her? Maybe it was only that. He liked her, respected her, maybe. She was a warrior woman, like his 'first love' and like his mother. She meant nothing else.

"I count four – no, five scars. I include the little scar on your cheek." She paused. "Is that your total?"

"You mean my back, do you, Cliro? By the Father, no, I haven't one on my back."

Her gaze left the alluring playground of his body and fastened on his blue eyes.

"Nor I."

"I didn't think so."

"I have more scars than you, Zem. Perhaps this shows me to have also lesser skill in battle."

"Or to be more brave? How many scars, then?"

"Seven."

One candle flickered, as if a spirit had breathed on it.

Neither of them looked at the candle.

He said in a low voice, "Show me."

And at his own words, his *thought*, Clirando beheld on him all the arousal any woman could ever have required.

It matched, she conceded, her own hidden want.

Her hands flew over her garments. She was bold, also flaunting. Her slim and tawny shape came from its concealment, the tips of her breasts already woken and hard.

In silence she pointed out the seven narrow scars – one on the right shoulder, three at her stomach and waist, two on her right leg, tiny as small coins, and the longest, deepest scar on her left arm, made by a blow that, in the moment it happened, she scarcely noted. It had been Araitha's in the war court.

The bed still lay between them. Divided by two swords.

"Cliro," he said, "be sure. If you have doubts, I'll take myself off into the inn. I do warn you, though, I shall then get myself very drunk."

"Stay sober. Stay with me."

As they moved about the bed to meet each other, each of them saw in a sudden glimpse one more magic, stranger and less strange than the sorcery of sex…

"The swords—"

Both blades had twined together, roping each other round like vines.

"Is that because we—?"

But he reached her then.

He took her face in his hands. His body gathered hers in. His mouth was familiar to her. She *knew* it, as if many times before…

All the inebriated power of sexual hunger coursed through her.

Her hands moved over his smooth and unmarked back. She gripped him against her.

In moments the entwined blades were thrust from the bed, and furs and coverlets in heaps across the floor.

His lips on her breasts were like a rain of warm honey, his teeth grazed her with shivering darts. At the flaming centre of her flesh he woke her fire into a conflagration.

They raced quickly along the road of lust, unable, either of them, to delay another minute.

As he filled her, her body sprang to amalgamate with his. The struggle of ecstasy began and exploded like every firecracker ever loosed on a night of full moon. Blind and moaning, they clung, the crescendo bursting them in an infinity of stopped time. Until, cradling each other, rocking, sighing, they fell back into the hollow of the night.

"We went too fast," he said.

"What else? I have waited."

"You waited for me. Did you know that?"

"But now you're here."

"Cliro," he said into her hair, as he lay on her, heavy, blissful, one cover she did not wish to push away.

They stayed like this for a short while, until she felt him stir again.

"Now we go more slowly," he said gravely.

And with his hands and mouth he played her, exquisite as any master musician, the strings of her body flowing with boundless notes. In an agony of joy, she held herself away from the brink. They rolled, still connected, and lying over him she now began to search out the melody of *his* flesh, tuning and waking him, torturing him to the peak of pleasure, casting herself over into the roiling sea only when she saw she had mastered him. The vast wave hurled them up again high as the moon, and over and slowly downward into the second valley of aftermath.

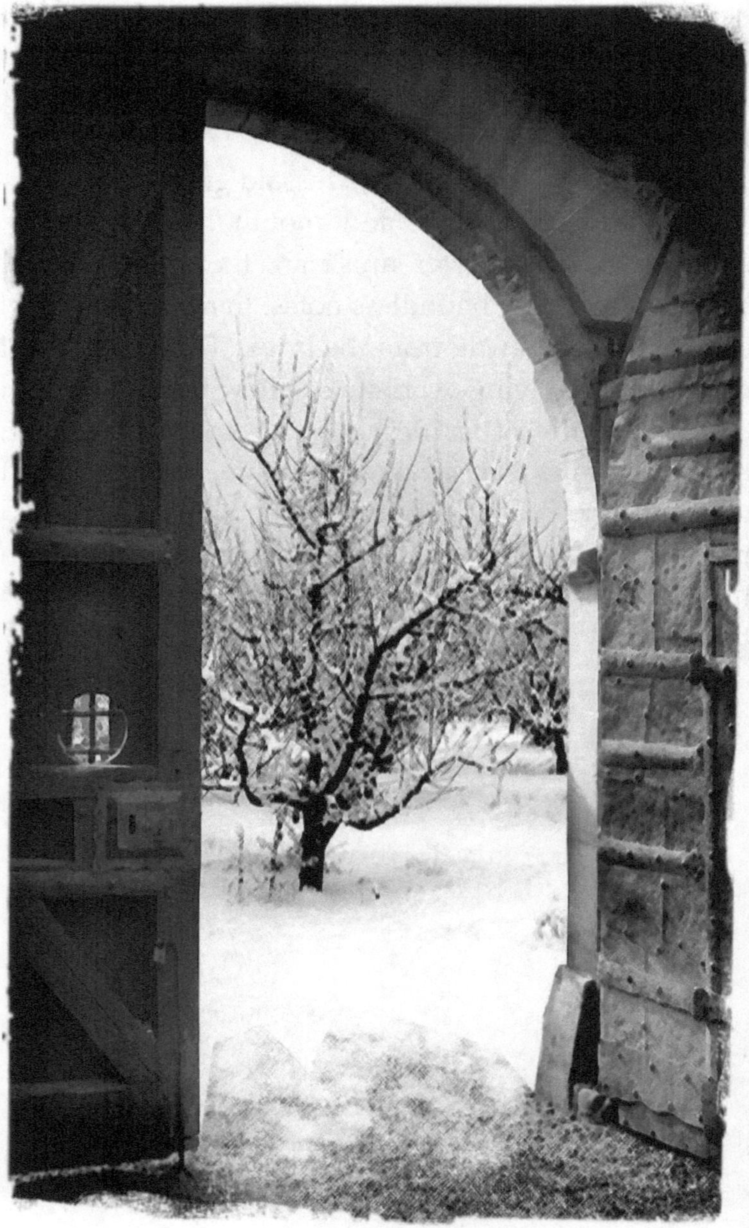

5.

WINTER

Clirando was cold. Winter – it was winter, and she lay outdoors. Where was she? Thestus lay by her, she could hear his deep sleeper's breathing. But she had slept as heavily, and now her skin seemed rimed with frost…

Clirando flung herself off the bed, panic-stricken, feral.

This was not Thestus. She was not on campaign. It was summer not winter.

She did not sleep.

Night's darkness was done with. A pallid, livid dawn was beginning over the village, and Clirando could make out how the sky was sombrely whitened, for she had left the shutters open. But this white sky was far too white. The roofs around were also *far too white.*

She went to the window. A blast of freezing air met her naked body like pain.

Small wonder. Heavy snow had fallen in the night. It covered everything – trees, buildings, and on the narrow alley below, undisturbed, it made a flawless marble paving.

Not a sound rose from the village, either. Not a trickle of smoke from any hastily stoked hearth. No bird flew. No human thing was visible. Under the deadly blossom of the snow and ice, only an intermittent conifer showed any growing covering. The rest of the trees were bare as bones, and on a nearby wall, an Eastern rose-briar snaggled, skeletal black and white. Last night it had been smothered in red flowers.

She heard Zemetrios erupt from the bed behind her.

"In the name of all—"

They wrapped themselves in the formerly redundant furs, and both stood in the window.

"The village is empty," he said. "Deserted."

"The village is *ruinous,*" Clirando added.

It was true. The more she peered at the icy vista, the more she noticed the holes in the plaster, fallen stones, and gaps where roofs had given way, not the previous night, but long ago. The snowy trees had not all been cultivated in gardens and yards, but had rooted in the houses, and out of streets and alleyways.

Even in this room—that crack along the wall, the broken stool she had not seen yesterday. The balding furs were musty with age.

Looking across the room, she dismally noted the old carven door was half off its hinges.

"The snow," he said with irony, "must have fallen down from the moon, if the moon's covered in snow as the man said."

"Perhaps it did. This place is a demonic trap. It's accursed, as we are."

He drew her around to face him.

"No longer. You and I are no more one alone to face the dangers and dirt of this world. Two together. Yes, Clirando?"

It did not go easy with her, even now, emotionally

to bond with him so quickly. If a summer morning had woken them, very likely she would have felt otherwise. But now once more she was not sure she could trust Zemetrios, her beautiful and mesmerising lover, the one she had 'waited' for, her equal and her beloved.

Nevertheless, she nodded. And saw in his eyes he knew she put him off that way. For a moment his mouth thinned. Turning from her brusquely, he gathered up his gear and began to dress.

No longer twined, their two swords lay among the quilts, separate.

Around and below, the inn was as void as suspected. In the long main room, under a now partly broken staircase, bushes clawed from the floor and icicles hung where the onions and green herbs once had. The smoke chimney had fallen into the cooking hearth – a hundred years ago from the look of it.

They exchanged very few words. Brief comments on the wreck, warnings about treacherous places in the floor, and in the snowy hollows of the streets and alleys outside, when once they got there.

The village was desolate, and desolating.

She – and he, she had believed – had been happy here, nearly carefree. The good food, the well-mannered crowds, and the music, magic, friendship, the potent law-breaking of the four magicians in the square – all of it lies. Hallucinations.

Traps.

Nothing to do with life or enjoyment had gone on in this winter village for ten decades or more, nothing but loneliness and decay. Not even any animal laired here.

And the snow. The snow. Could it had fallen from the snow-covered midsummer moon? Was that likely – of course not. But then, neither was all the rest.

We were lovers. This demonstrates we were fools, after all. Or I was a fool. And he, trustless, one more chancer and traitor.

For once a kinder inner voice, perhaps more rational – or less guilt-ridden, less *involved* – murmured within her: *Do you react too harshly? What, after all, has he done that you should call him by such names?*

But winter had shown her, with its unseasonal cruelty, that she must not soften. She had trusted before. Now she must raise her shield if not her blade. She must be forearmed.

They emerged from the village at another gate. In fact out of a hole in the wall.

Looking back, Clirando saw the remains of the slender tower, leaning like a smashed tooth on the sky.

Beyond the 'gateway' was only a waste of white, in which groups of dead orchard trees huddled like black cages draped with ice.

The mountains rose ahead. They were solid now in snow, and the white land ran up to them. Pine forest still grew thickly at their bases.

"Moon's Stair," Zemetrios said. His voice was bleak.

Clirando scanned the middle peak.

It was not so high as she had thought, only a frigid hump. Who would want to go up there?

"Everything was deception," she said. "The merchant lied, too. How can there be some supernatural doorway on that mountain that allows men to pass through and walk on the moon's globe – if a globe it truly even is. The moon is a lamp, that's all, like the stars. The gods made them simply to give light."

"In Rhoia," he said, "we call the moon most often *she*. She's frozen. She's cold. Unjust. A bringer of regret."

Clirando flung about. Before she could make some hard rejoinder, she thought confusedly, *he spoke of the moon. He was not Thestus taunting me.*

A wind woke suddenly from the island's edges, where, invisible, the sea still coiled, its rim perhaps now layered with ice.

"What's that sound?" he said.

"The wind blowing."

"No."

He pointed.

Along the snow, out of the nearest bundle of pine trees, something came striding with huge steps. On all the white it was night-dark. And it was giant – tall but narrow, a black banner blowing like a black flame from its top.

"The woman on stilts," Clirando exclaimed.

"So it is."

They waited.

Such was her speed, the striding stilt-walker reached them in less than a minute.

Last night she had lit torches in a ruin that had looked whole and living.

Now, passing them, the apparition bent her head to regard them.

"Moon's Stair," said the black woman in a remote

tone. "That's your path."

"Why?" Zemetrios shouted up at her.

"Why else?" the woman nonsensically said.

She grinned. Her teeth were white as winter. On she strode, around the crumbled village wall. She vanished from sight.

"A sign," he said. "Guidance."

"Only if you're insane enough to think it so. I'm making back the other way toward the coast. My band of women was abducted by pirates, that's what I must suppose. At Amnos, to be a female warrior is to be a priestess, too. I owe them more than mere comradeship – they were in my charge. So, damn the Isle and the Seven Nights. I'll build a beacon of my own and hail some ship. I must find them."

"Clirando," he said, "don't you see, you and I – *we* must go up the mountain."

"Why should I see something so absurd."

"Our penance. Didn't your temple speak to you of a sacrifice?"

Clirando stared at nothingness. "Yes. They said too that there was less danger for my girls than for me."

"I'd swear your band is safe. They're valiant and strong. You've trained and led them. So you must trust them, even if you can never trust me. As for this – don't you feel the tug of that place – whatever it is... up there?"

She licked her lips. The chill wind was biting through her clothing and the moulting furs in which she, as he, had wrapped herself.

Unwillingly she accepted that it was true enough, the mountain pulled at her. It was not so high. It would be no awful task for either of them to scale it.

Instantly on the wind, then, she heard a many-voiced and horrible jeering wail. As her head jerked up in remembering fear and distaste, she saw Zemetrios too was glaring along the snows, his eyes searching. Their demons had returned.

There had been a sip of happiness for them at the phantom inn. Now they were due to pay.

"Then, let's go," he said. "What choice?"

"None."

He broke into the fast, steady lope before she did, running toward the skirt of pines.

It would not matter, she thought, despite any prior notion or hope, whether they went together or apart. Both of them must face the individual punishment the Isle had in store.

Yet she too jogged forward. Increasing her speed, she caught him up. They advanced again shoulder to shoulder, up the rising slope.

6.

MOON

All that day they climbed. Once they were through the hedge of pines, the mountain was not itself irksome, but the slides of impacted snow and translucent ice sometimes presented blocks to swift progress.

They began, inadvertently, to work as a team.

Bittersweet, this. Clirando had never met a man so sane in his judgment of obstacles or so decided in solving them. Nor, where she detected the solution, so willing to agree. She had found many men in the past, even some of the best, obstreperous as it were on principle. Thestus primarily. She would have understood this if she had been a house-reared woman, but she was educated, trained, fit, and canny.

Where necessary, they assisted each other.

They took only short breaks from the ascent. Neither had any food, and only a little water, which they drank sparingly.

Once he remarked that the previous evening's dinner had seemed to nourish them, even if it had been sorcerous and non-existent.

At this she recalled again the other feast – the sexual and emotional feast of their lovemaking.

She saw that he did, too.

He said, looking at her, "My name you know. It was never Thestus."

Rage boiled in her, then died.

"I know. But let that be for now."

And silence returned to divide them as two swords had not.

Twilight, after the unseen sun went down, found them high on the shelves of Moon's Stair.

A broad cave, one of many, yawned in the mountain. They ducked in and made a fire.

"Who watches?" he asked.

"I."

"Last night you slept."

"That was some spell. I shan't tonight."

"Do you think so?"

Presently they portioned the watch, in the acceptable way, between them, lying or sitting far across the fire from each other.

The full moon of the Third Night swam up the sky, only partly tearing the veil of snow-cloud. Later, more snow fluttered down.

How beautiful he was, asleep.

A rift of tenderness opened in her heart. She slammed a mental door against it.

Clirando did not slumber. When he took the watch, she lay static as a log, her back to him.

Outside, at frequent intervals, and as she had heard it during the slog up the mountain, there echoed the dim jeering yodels of the pig things, her personal demons. He presumably heard the abusive shouts of his dead friend and brother, Yazon.

It was not that she dreamed, but she had one brief almost-vision of Araitha. Clirando's own friend and sister floated through the depths of a dark sea, a corpse with golden hair furling and unfurling.

Next morning, they drank the last water, some of which was by then ice, and went out.

Inside an hour of traveling, the way flattened to a craggy, endless-seeming plateau. They had gained the top of Moon's Stair.

They paused. Snow armoured the crag. Outcrops thrust white into the dead sky. Boulders lay everywhere. There was nothing unusual, but also nothing comfortable up here. It was a place of the known earth, yet *alien* – as only the things of the earth could be.

"There was after all no purpose in climbing here."

"Nevertheless, we climbed," he said. "Everything in life is like that, surely. It's our choice and talent to make a purpose from such chaos."

The wind lifted and fell, cutting about itself with sharp blades.

Into the lea of one of the outcrops they went, for shelter.

Below, far off, slopes, forest, the lost village. It was just possible too, she thought, even in the wan daylight, to imagine the mighty outer circle of ocean ringing the island.

By nightfall they had trekked some way over the mountaintop. They sought a crevice between rocks for the night's bivouac.

Tomorrow they would descend. There was nothing else to do.

The moon came up in the dark. This evening it was

unclouded, shining on the snow.

It was the Fourth Night. The middle night of the seven.

Clirando again took first watch.

In order this time not to gaze at him in his sleep, she stared rigidly out across the fire.

An hour later, in the moonlight and with no warning, Araitha came walking toward Clirando over the mountain.

Clirando got up. She drew her knife – pointlessly.

Araitha wore her travelling cloak, and in her hair were the ornaments she had put there for safekeeping during her voyage to Crentis. No doubt in reality they lay with her on the sea's floor.

Lovely, strong, brave – how proud you could be of her, this ghost. Comrade – friend – sister…

"Stay back, dead thing," rasped Clirando. "Only say what you want from me."

Araitha did not slow her pace. She sighed, and her ghost-breath, clean as when she had lived, touched Clirando's face.

Clirando thought the ghost would keep going until it walked right through her. She gripped her knife and braced herself – but at the last second Araitha dissolved like coloured steam.

Yet, in the open area beyond the rocks, everything now was changed.

The mountain plateau was no longer there.

A vast blank alabaster whiteness loomed and curved away. It was not snow, but level, even, and icy *cold* with a burnish like freezing fire. While above, contrastingly, the sky was an inky black Clirando had never witnessed on any other night. Stars *seared* on this black like volcanic embers, and of all shades – purple, russet, amber, jade. But the moon itself had disappeared. Instead, hanging low over a distant jumble of countless spiked mountains – as unlike those of the Isle as was possible – *another* moon shone. In colour it was greenish turquoise. It cast an underwater light and formed peculiar shadows. Soon Clirando did not think it was a moon. It was some other – lamp? *World*? Or was it in fact the earth, hung in the sky off the moon itself?

She found she had stolen forward. She felt no startlement, only a dull terror when, turning, she saw even the rocks from which she had just emerged were now no longer behind her. All the mountain was gone now. On every side, the white sheer surface ran to its horizon.

She took a breath. Very oddly, it seemed to her the air here was not air at all – and still her lungs expanded. She thought, *I am on the moon's world now. Or some part of me…* She did not know which part, nor how she breathed that which was not air. But she did. For she was not meant to perish yet, oh no. Araitha, vindictive, had undone the barrier between the worlds, and Clirando had been sucked through.

The shadows though – they moved.

They slithered forward, growing solid as they did so – be ready!

They are not shadows.

How many of them were there? It was a herd, a *battalion* of the blackish pig creatures, tusked and spined, their misshapen heads lolling, glassy little eyes riveted on her.

Before she could do anything at all, they had pressed inward, forming a circle about her. She was surrounded. Two or three animals deep, the live cordon wobbled on narrow feet, grunting, snuffling. Until at last the familiar hideous jeering screams broke from them, deafening now and no longer weirdly synchronised, but all out of rhythm.

Clirando hissed in fury. It thrust out her fear.

Knife in hand, she flew at her tormentors. She raked and slashed them. She felt the blows strike home. She saw the blood spurt burningly red in the uncanny light. They did not resist, nor did they attack – but the jeering cacophony never ceased.

All around the circle she pelted, and around again. Still not one of the black pigs retaliated. None harmed her. She stopped all at once, panting, somehow disabled… Each blow had lessened her.

And only then the circle gradually fell quiet.

After the unbearable horror of the noise, the *un*-air of this second world congealed inside her ears. It was as if she had gone deaf…

And *now* they must close in. She had hurt them. They would trample her and kill her. Eat her alive.

Clirando straightened. She could sell her life expensively, even if she must sacrifice it in the end.

And so she saw.

It was like a blindfold dropping from her eyes.

The creatures stood there quite motionless and still making no sound. They were striped and running with blood. Much worse than this, from their greenish eyes enormous glittering tears poured down like rain.

Crying, they clustered in their circle, and they looked at her. And as Clirando stared into their weeping eyes, she saw through to the backs of these eyes, as if through polished mirrors, and then straight down to some other thing, repeating, amplifying, which she could not make out.

"Why do you do this?" she whispered.

They only wept.

Clirando took now a few tentative steps. She approached the nearest of them.

It lifted its head. It was ugly, terrible, pitiable. The crying seemed to have made its eyes much larger. They were deeply green, like the leaves of a bay tree.

Memory flashed in Clirando's brain. Her mother was picking her up from the courtyard, where she had fallen, a Clirando then about four years old. "Don't cry, my love."

"Don't cry, my love," Clirando murmured.

She found she had dropped the knife. She put out both her hands and touched the pig's nightmare face quite gently. "Don't cry. It will be better soon."

To her bewilderment, the pig at once nuzzled in close to her. It was warm. It smelled healthy and wholesome, but not really animal. Her hands slid over it. It had no spines after all. It was smooth. Under her fingers, the wetness of the blood, the wounds she had caused, healed like seams sewn together.

Now the next animal was nudging at her. Eagerly?

"Come here," said Clirando.

She had shut her eyes.

She took the second pig into her arms.

She took all of them into her arms, one by one. She

stroked them. She kissed their bizarre faces; she kissed the tears away and their wounds healed.

All this, with her eyes shut.

She too was crying, she discovered. And then, softly laughing. And from the pigs as she went around to them, embracing them, soft laughter, too.

She knew when she had reached the end of her ministrations and closed the fateful circle. That was when she opened her eyes.

Twenty or thirty other Clirandos stood all about her. They were her age, and her height and weight, clothed as she was under the furs, in summer garments, tanned and fit, shaking back brown hair.

The pig-creature had been – herself? No, no – *facets* of herself. Her *self.*

Jeering, tormenting – *ugly*.

Was this then what she really was? Or what, deep in her mind, her heart, she had *believed* she was?

If so, then she had mocked herself, and driven herself, *hurt* herself, made herself *weep* if not actual tears, then *symbolic* tears. To lose love was a very terrible thing. To lose affection for one's own self – this must be worse. For you could, at least in your mind, move far off from others. But from yourself you never could, until death released you.

She regarded the other Clirandos, and they her. Clear-eyed, these looks, and mouths that did not laugh, calm mouths, quiet.

They were separated from her, her other selves. Her anger, and her attempt to suppress anger, both, had done this. And her pain and her denial of that pain. For pain and anger needed to be felt and to be expressed –

and then let go.

She tried to count them, the other Clirandos. Twenty – thirty – ten – she could not get the number to come out.

But she had split herself into these pieces. She thought of a mirror made of glass, as they formed them in the East – shattered.

Clirando bowed her head. Anger was spoken. Pain acknowledged. Both now must begin their journey away from her. She visualised a glass mirror, mending...

Did she feel her other selves return? Perhaps – perhaps. When she raised her head, they were gone. Only she remained. But all of her now, she thought, all mended and in one piece.

And so when, next moment, she saw rushing across the moon's long vista, the dappled lion-beast she had first seen on the cliffs of the Isle, she did not draw her knife. Now, she *knew*.

As it sprang, she too sprang forward.

In space they met. The collision was instantaneous and had no impact, only a brilliant lightning that coursed through her, cold then hot, then warm.

Landing in a warrior's practiced crouch, Clirando knew herself for one moment to be a dappled lynx-lion, tail lashing, claws ready, eyes of fire. And then the beast sank back into her spirit, accustomed as a fine knife in a sheath of velvet.

The male lion also had been – was – hers. It was a part of her. She had no need to dread it, only to know and guide it – and permit it, at the correct times, to guide her.

A joy beyond all joys filled Clirando. She ran about

the moon plain, jumped high, whirled through the air, light as a feather, playing.

Never had she known such liberation. But even as she experienced it, intuitively she recognised it could not and must not last. Mortals had their duties in the world. Only before and after death could such freedom deservedly be theirs.

She sat thinking this for a while, there on the surface of the moon, quite calm. Until something altered in her mind, and suddenly she began to see instead her ridiculous predicament. For she knew no route back. If a psychic gate had been opened for her, where was it now? She did not think the ghost of Araitha could conduct her home into the world.

The surreal euphoria had left her. Perplexed, Clirando stood and looked away to all the white horizons.

Vaguely then, she heard a distant shouting. It was no longer any nightmare of her own.

Zemetrios…?

Had he too been pulled through to this other place, to contend with his past?

At this thought Clirando became fully herself – or reckoned she did. In the heat of battle, you could not always carefully plan.

It took her some hours to walk across the long curving of the moon's back, and the fish-bone spikes of the mountains were much nearer when she halted in astonishment.

Before her lay a fine house, that would have fitted well in the upper streets of Amnos. It was surrounded by a grove of trees, winter bare and thick with icicles. The house seemed to think an ordinary earthly night had fallen, for lamplight burned in the visible windows and over the gate of the courtyard. The gate itself was ajar, as if to invite Clirando in.

She hesitated. But then the strident shouting came again. She had heard it many times as she travelled; it had guided her here.

She pushed wide the gate and crossed the yard, between ranks of frozen urns and shrubs.

The door of the house too was open.

Clirando entered, sword in hand, and reached the threshold of a graciously furnished room now rather spoilt. A chair had gone over. Broken pitchers lay on the floor. Two men were there also, one of them stumbling, shouting. It was this awful voice she had heard before.

Then, in the moment before the shouting stumbler fell, the other man caught him back. "Yazon, listen to me. This would have been your twenty-ninth day without drunkenness. Think what you had achieved."

"And lost," the other grated. "I have ruined it. Besides, what do I care? Give it me back, the wine…" But Yazon's voice dropped away into sobs. He sank down on a couch.

And Zemetrios seated himself beside him. "No, my friend. No wine. You'll have to kill me first." Zemetrios. His face was weary as that of a man who had been entirely sleepless for months, yet also hard and resolute.

Yazon – he could be no one else – was speaking now of horrible secrets of drunkenness. But his eyes at last were growing sane and sad.

As if some god had told her – Sattu, perhaps, the little god of domestic things – Clirando seemed to know it all.

This naturally was not what had taken place in the world, at Rhoia. Instead, the house of Zemetrios's father had been magically rebuilt here on the slopes of the moon, by some spirit or spell. And now, in this new reality, Zemetrios – having given up his post in the king's legions and sent all his servants, women and men both, away to safety – cared for Yazon, striving to cure him, to make him whole.

That then must have been in Zemetrios's hidden mind. Not that he had killed Yazon in rage – but that he had not devoted his life, however briefly or lengthily, to helping Yazon. Not with money or shelter, but with the comradeship and dedication they had each shown the other in war. Now Zemetrios wished to atone.

It was very plain that Zemetrios believed utterly this situation truly existed.

Clirando did not know if she could, or should, have any part in such a scenario. But the previous bliss of her own liberation now filled her with the desire to assist in whatever way was possible. To assist, that was, Zemetrios.

She spoke his name. Could he hear her?

Yes. He looked across at her instantly. His face, which had seemed older than its twenty-four years, was suddenly as she recalled. A smile lit his mouth and eyes.

"And here is my beautiful wife, Clirando."

The other man – ghost – illusion – whatever he might be – also looked up at her. And he too gave her a smile. It was not corrupt, only distant. Some half-forgotten good manners from an earlier time when he had been himself. And she wondered then if perhaps really this was Yazon, come back from death to undo this knot of pain and anger, as needful for his phantasmal life as it was for Zemetrios's mortal one.

"And I warn you, Yazon," said Zemetrios, with amused lightness, "try nothing stupid with her. She'll kill you and have your skin sewn up as a sunshade."

His *wife*.

In his fantasy, this dream of righting wrongs and making all good, I am his wife...

Zemetrios got up, came to her and kissed her gently on the lips. "Things will be better now you're here."

Only Clirando marked accurately the passing of the last three nights of full moon. Though perhaps she did not do it as accurately as she meant to, because she had to get her bearings from the rise and fall of the blue-green earth-world above.

In the house, apparently, months went by.

She herself was not conscious of these. Her time frame functioned very differently, and the scenes that were enacted, and in which she sometimes took a small part, were fragments of some vaster drama, played clearly for Zemetrios alone.

She went along with everything, knowing he did what he must. His penance and self-examination were longer than hers, deeper and darker though less savage.

In the segments of events that Clirando witnessed,

Zemetrios hauled Yazon back to sober health. Zemetrios was by turns dominant and consoling, as appropriate. He never gave up, and gradually the physical ghost-image of Yazon responded. Then Clirando would find the two of them at friendly, noisy practice with swords or bows, or wrestling, eating, talking. They played Lybirican chess. They would discuss the army days and reminisced away the nights that somehow came and went inside the outer time which she alone observed. They would look up at the blue orb in the sky and call it the moon.

Of course, Zemetrios never separately sought her. It seemed she was tucked away somewhere in his illusory life in the house. Mainly, she was peripheral to his task. Sometimes he did not even see or hear her as she entered a room only a few paces from him. He only ever fully saw Yazon, the one in fact who probably was not there.

She began to think Yazon was not a ghost, working out the dilemma of its life. No, he was solely a conjuring of Zemetrios's mind. And of Moon Isle.

She came to believe all this would end at the finish of the moon's Seventh Night. Till then she could do nothing but be present, offering her slight participation – a touch, a cup filled from the well in the courtyard. Every illusory thing seemed real, as in the village. Therefore, how would this saga be resolved?

She pondered too with the winter snow in her heart, if Zemetrios would have been driven mad by the finish of it.

The ultimate problem was their return to the world, which still she had not solved. Maybe they must stay here, despite all expiation. And maybe too they would be segregated here from each other.

Do I love him?

Even in that extremity and strangeness, this question was paramount, and unanswered.

Sometimes she sat alone in the winter yard of the simulated Rhoian house, gazing up at the multi-coloured stars. Indoors the men talked rationally, remembering old campaigns.

The food and drink she had found in the kitchens had nourished her, and them. Even the rug bed she had made herself was comfortable. She could sleep now. Anywhere, therefore, would have been comfortable.

Perhaps madness has taken all of us.

But the lion lashed its tail in her spirit, and she herself quieted it. *Be patient.*

When next the blue orb rose, that would be the Seventh Night, as far as she knew. She could do nothing but wait.

In sleep, she heard Zemetrios speaking to her very softly. "It's done, Cliro. He has gone."

Instantly she was fully awake. "Where?"

"Away. Away where he must."

He spoke of Yazon. Who, it seemed, had gone back to the lands beyond death.

Zemetrios said, "This has been a dream."

She thought, *thank all gods, he knows.*

"But it was a dream I needed to be dreaming. Oh, Clirando, I should have given him that, no matter how he was. I should have tried so much harder to save him, in the true world, while he lived. Not dragged him into my house and shunned and treated him like a sinful baby, despised and left him always to himself, busy with my own affairs. I should not either have gone out and left my servants at his mercy – afraid of him, afraid to offend *me*.

"I've done what I should have done, but here. It's – freed me. But I shall never cease to be sorry." He leaned close to her, resting his forehead on hers. "How long has all this gone on? It seemed a year… But he was my friend, my brother… Oh, Cliro – if only I'd done this *then*, as I should."

She held him. They lay wrapped among the rugs, like two children in the dark. "Hush, my love," she said. "If only any of us had done what we should. We see it clearly when it has passed by. Yet we must try to see and try to do. That's all the gods ask. That we try."

And she thought, *and is he my love, then?*

And she thought, *yes, he is my love.*

They curled together. Beyond the narrow window the blue disk gemmed the sky.

He had survived the test and was not deranged. Each of them had paid their debt to themselves. They slept exhausted in each other's arms.

The next time they woke, it was together, and they lay on the bare plains of the moon. The house with all its lamps and groves, its rooms and well and yard, was gone. Only those mountains like spines scratched along the horizon.

The earth hung above, and all the stars.

"There was a way that led us here, beyond the

rocks," he said. "But how do we find it?"

Clirando stared into her mind. There were visions there still, things which came from the magic not only of this place, but from the sorcery of the Isle.

Slowly she said, "There's home," nodding at the disk above.

"But the *way* to it?"

Clirando's brain showed her the magicians in the square who had called the stars.

Instinctively, she raised her arms.

Up in the inky black, the exquisite jewellery shivered. One by one, stars – *stars* – detached from their moorings. They began to float down, not a swarm now, a snowfall…

If it was a dream, you might do anything. And if not, still you might attempt it.

The stars wove around one another in slow, sparkling tidal surges. She thought of the old woman weaving on the headland, the old man who made snakes at the forest's end, and of the stilt-walker lighting torches.

High in the air, a bridge began to form in a wide, swooping arc. It was laid with coruscating stellar stones – emeralds, rubies, amethysts – it curved down toward the surface where they stood, making a hill road for them to climb. While the rest of the arc soared away like the curve of a bow. Infinities up in the air, the earth disk had received the far point of this incredible bridge, without the tiniest ripple.

They neither debated nor held back. Both he and she ran at the bridge of stars, this extraordinary path that led toward the ordinary, and the mortal.

Simultaneously they leaped, landed. Clirando felt the faceted paving under her feet. Ethereal colours washed them like high waters, now copper, now bronzy, now golden.

Not to sleep so long – it had been worth it, to know a dream like this one.

Both of them laughed. Children laughed like that, innocent, and prepared to credit that dreams came true.

As so often on the Isle, shoulder to shoulder, Clirando and Zemetrios broke into their companionable, well-trained, mile-eating lope. Over the night, over the heavens, running home through the spatial outer dark which, for them, was full of a rich sweet air, mild breezes, summery scents, branches of static stars, rainbows and light, wild music, half-seen winged beings.

Clirando knew no fear, no doubt, and no reticence. She thought idly, as she bounded earthward, *this is the truth.*

But somewhere, something – oh, it was like a vagrant cloud, feathery and adrift. It bloomed out from nowhere. It poured around her. Zemetrios was concealed. She half turned, missing him, and then a delicate nothingness enveloped her. That too brought no alarm. It was also too good, too *true.*

And after only a second anyway it was done.

And then—

"Clirando!"

This known female face bending to hers, someone well liked, familiar…

"Tuyamel?"

Clirando's eyes were clearing. She stared into six faces now, all known, all in their way loved. Her girls, the women of her band.

"Lie still, Cliro," said Tuy firmly. "You've flown such a great way off and had such a long journey back."

They were sworn to secrecy, they assured her, all of them. No one who came here must ever afterward speak of the secrets of Moon Isle. Besides, they knew very little.

"Certain persons – they go to certain places. The priests – and the gods – direct them. Some even go – so we heard – to the moon itself. And you went somewhere, Cliro. That's what they said."

Her band told her how, the morning after they had beached their boat on the strand of the Isle, they had found her unconscious, and had not been able to rouse her. Though she breathed, she seemed all but dead. And so they picked her up on a litter improvised from cloaks, and bore her inland.

An ancient priestess by a beacon on the cliff top declared Clirando had suffered no awful harm. "She has not slept a while," the priestess said. "Now she must."

So Clirando's loyal girls carried her, with much care and attention, to one of the seven inland villages of the island.

"Every night of the full moon you lay here," lamented Seleti.

"We tried to wake you – the moon *was* full for seven nights!" – Draisis – "But you never stirred."

"And the old priest, the one with the pet snakes he names after jewels – he said we must let you slumber. You were so young, he said," affrontedly added Erma, "you would certainly see in your lifetime several more such seasons of seven moons."

"You missed all the festivities," elaborated Oani.

"Jugglers – magicians…" Vlis.

"One of them made a bridge over the sky, all like precious stones – green, red, mauve, yellow…" Tuyamel. "Though *I* knew it was all a trick."

Clirando lay on the narrow pallet, in the cell of the temple in Seventh Village.

Her heart beat leadenly.

It had been – *all* of it – a dream?

And yet, she had been enabled to throw away the negative and hateful things. Only proper grief and regret remained. Except... Zemetrios.

If all this had been a dream – including even, as it had, transcripts of actual external things – what had *Zemetrios* been? His thoughts, his personality – his mouth, his arms?

She lay a few days in the little Temple of the Maiden. Then, when she had recovered enough, Clirando roamed through its courts, admiring columns and the flowering vines on its walls – for summer had continued uninterrupted in the world. Here and there, meeting others, she mentioned a particular name.

"Zemetrios?" they asked, the mild priestesses.

"Warrior," they said to her, not unkindly, "no one may be told anything more than the minimum of any other here. This is Moon Isle. For those like yourself, or the man you mention, what each does and experiences is a private matter. Only they and the gods can know."

So they would tell her nothing. And was there anything to learn?

Everything else had been her dream, so why not this golden man? She had wanted a lover. Tranced or asleep, she had had one.

And now she knew for sure she loved him? Well, then. She loved a figment of her dreams. She would not be the first or last.

Two days following the celebration of the Seven Nights, which all of them repeatedly reminded her she had missed, Clirando walked around the village.

It was not at all like the one she had seen when asleep. The buildings were clean and garishly painted. The three or four temples were garlanded, and that of the Maiden had walls of deep red, patterned with silver crescents.

Just as she had heard, priests and priestesses thronged the Isle, and lingering warrior bands were there, too traders and performers, but now the processions and shows were over. A great packing up was going on. A great leave-taking.

And neither was it any use to question these people, let alone the villagers, who seemed educated in coy evasions. There seemed too a polite, unspoken wish that visitors should go. It began to make her band uneasy, and soon enough Clirando, as well.

I threw off my guilt. I must throw off this also.

She slept always soundly at night. She did not dream, she thought, at all, as if she had used all her dreaming up. Would she ever see the ghost of Araitha again? Or him – would she ever see Zemetrios again? No. Never.

On the fourth day they set off along the forest track. It was rather as Clirando had visualised it, but then her girls had carried her this way. Now animals and birds abounded. A statue marked either end of the road, island gods, nicely carved. Clirando thrust her introspection from her. She acted out being her ordinary self, calling it back to her. It came.

Meanwhile her girls were so attentive and careful of her that Clirando eventually lost her temper. "Leave off treating me like some fragile shard of ancient pottery! What will you do on the boat? Wrap a shawl over my legs and pat me on the head?"

There under the sun-sparkling pines, she wrestled Tuyamel and Vlis, and threw them both, and hugged them all. They danced about there, laughing, embracing, loud and boisterous as eleven-year-olds.

Next day they reached the shore and rowed out to the galley. By sunfall they were on the way to Amnos, and life as they remembered it.

EPILOGUE

PAPER

The windblown sky was full of birds that morning.

Summer had stayed late in Amnos, giving way at last to a harsh, bleached winter.

Now spring tides freshened the coast, and men and beasts were casting the torpor of the cold months.

Clirando had been with Eshti, her old servant woman, to the fish market, and coming back Eshti bolted straight to the kitchen with her prizes. Clirando climbed up to the roof of her house. She was watching the antics of the house doves circling over the courtyard trees.

And out of her inner eyes, from nowhere, Araitha came, and stood silent in her mind. Clirando recalled how she had stood in the yard too laying her curse, then turning away from shadow to light to shadow– or had it been light to shadow to light...?

Unlike her companion, her dream lover, Clirando had had no dialogue with her dead friend to set anything right between them.

Araitha therefore might always haunt her. No longer injurious, only bitter. It could not be helped. At least her curse was spent.

All winter Clirando had carried on her life as she had in the past. If her mood was sometimes uneven, she hid it. Mourning the loss of a dead comrade was one thing, but to mourn the loss of someone who had not been *real* was wretched and bewildering. Sometimes she even mocked herself. But now – `now it was spring.

Clirando turned. Eshti had come up on the roof, puffing from the steps, wiping fish scales off on her apron.

"What now?" Clirando inquired. "Has dinner swum away?"

"No, lady. The priestesses of Parna have sent for you."

Clirando's thoughts scattered apart and back together in concern. She sprang downstairs to fetch her cloak.

In the shrine by the main temple hall, one of the two priestesses who received Clirando was the middle-aged woman who had dispatched her to the Isle.

Clirando saluted both of them. She said, "Have I committed some error, Mothers?"

The two of them gazed at Clirando. Only the older priestess smiled. "Not at all. There are matters which have just come to our attention. Now spring has driven the ice from the harbours, ships are moving, and letters have arrived in Amnos."

Clirando nodded. Though familiar with books, she had seldom seen a letter. Next moment she saw two. Normally they would be of folded cloth, written on, then waxed, Both of these letters were of fine paper, made from Lybirican reeds.

"A ship's captain brought them here this morning," said the other priestess. "One is for you, Clirando. The other..."

"The other was sent to us by one of the Wise Women of Moon Isle. She is over a hundred years of age, but she lives sometimes in a hut on a headland, and still she weaves cloth, for her eyes stay clear and her fingers agile."

"I met her," said Clirando. She checked. "Or thought I did."

"The Wise Woman – she has no other name – says that something has come to her notice about a warrior girl, Clirando she is called, who was sent to the Isle to work out some inner tussle. The gods allowed her the trance of profound sleep, which the Isle can give, and in the sleep various adventures, by means of which her trouble was healed. However," the priestess paused. And Clirando's heart paused within her. "It seems, during this time, Clirando showed strong evidence of being herself a healer and a spiritual guide."

Shocked, Clirando interrupted. "*No,* Mother – I did nothing like that..."

Ignoring her, gently the priestess went on, "Although personal experiences on the Isle are not generally spoken of, there are two exceptions to this rule. Firstly, as perhaps you will guess, anyone may speak in secret to a priest of their own experience. This recital may naturally include mention of others who have – or who have seemed to have – been part of it. The priests, though they will answer no direct question, will nevertheless, should it be needful, afterwards pass on any insight to those others who have shared the event, providing, and this is the second exception, the insight is sufficiently profound. And so: A man, a soldier formerly with the Rhoian legions, reported the events to the Temple of the Father on the Isle. He too had been sent there to work out some penance and guilt and sorrow, and he too had the god's trance fall on him. The priests cared for him in this sleep, as it is always done, just as the priestesses cared for you, Clirando. But when he woke, he had an unusual story to tell. It seems he found himself in a forest, and there he met a young woman, who engaged his interest at once, being, he freely says, for him the perfect type of woman, both a warrior and a girl of great grace."

The priestess smiled again, peered into one of the paper letters, and read aloud: "Also blessed with a passionate clear mindedness."

The priestess allowed the letter to fall closed once more. "It seems too, that in this dream he had, and which apparently he shared with her, the woman he describes so admiringly – and whose name he gives as Clirando – that she gave him to understand she was not averse to his person. At the conclusion of their journey, she assisted him further, guiding him forward, as he describes, through a magical gateway, and so onto the mystic plains of the moon itself. Here his own difficulty was resolved, but once again Clirando remained at his side, helping him always. Now, we hear of visits to the moon, which may happen on the Isle – how else did it come by its name? – but they are rare. He insists that, had it not been for the woman, he himself would never have got there, and so never confronted what he must. Finally, when all was done, she..." the priestess again consulted the paper "...summoned a path of stars and led him home by that route to the world. But – to his horror – he lost her on the way."

The priestess folded the paper into her sleeve. She looked at Clirando. "Do you know anything of this?"

Clirando could not speak.

Then words came. "He is called Zemetrios?"

"So he is. I note your heart is full of love for him. That is the Maiden's gift to you, then. But it takes much more than love alone to work the magic you have done, my girl. And so it transpires the Maiden gave you another gift, too. For you are a healer and guide, as he has said. No, don't shake your head. Of course you have made mistakes and blunders on this occasion. It was your first excursion into such realms. You will need training, as tough and demanding as any you've known in the fighter's art. You stumbled on your gift, which till now you never knew you had. But this man Zemetrios is no fool. He insists you possess psychic powers. He has convinced the Wise Women. That's enough for us. Such talents must never be denied."

"Then..."

"Then, as I've said, you shall be taught. You will still be a warrior, but to one trade will be added another."

"But... Mother... I..."

"Now, sit on the bench there and read this second letter, which has come only for you. The ship's captain has said he wishes a moment with you, then. He's in the Little Fountain Courtyard. No doubt he expects to be rewarded for bringing such costly paper all this distance."

Clirando found she had sat down. She sat with the second letter unopened. All she could see or think was filled only by one face, one name. He was real, he lived, and knew her. She had guided him unknowing through forest and mountain and otherworld, her lover, her beloved, Zemetrios. And their lovemaking – though experienced in a dream – had in some manner taken place, for both. Yet now… he mentioned nothing of meeting her again…

The flame flicked before the statue of the goddess.

Her green eyes blinked, or it was only a trick of the light.

Clirando broke the wax seal on the second letter, her mind blank as a paper never written on.

And read this:

They will have told you I'm dead. But I did not drown when the Lion sank. The waves and wind dragged me to shore, with two or three others from the ship, and washed us up senseless at a little fisher village. Most of a year I stayed there, making a slow recovery, but a complete one. At last I set out and reached Sippini. From the port there I write to you now. I am in good health and strong again and have engaged with a warrior band to fight honourably for the town. My former disgrace I confessed, but they have overlooked it, saying both you, and the gods, had given me a beating and let me off. Now I might turn to better things.

Clirando, be aware that I acknowledge now the miserable wrong I did you. I hadn't any need to lie down with Thestus and should have resisted myself and him. For this mean act I lost your friendship always. Nor do I plead that you will change your mind, for I deserve nothing else. But the other crime I worked against you... Oh, Clirando, I regret that almost worse. To curse you – you that I wronged. At least I know that such a petty thing would never stick – it can never have harmed you, you are so strong. But I am ashamed. Forgive me, Clirando, if you are ever able, for both my faults. And think sometimes one kind thought, in tribute to our happier past, of me...

Once your sister and comrade,
Araitha

The letter fluttered from Clirando's fingers. The motion reminded her of a dove's wings.

Araitha lived. Araitha lived and was herself again. A hot blameless joy burned through Clirando. Standing up, she cried aloud, there in the shrine, naming the gods. It was not blasphemy, but a paean of gratitude. As such, it seemed, the goddess Parna at least received it.

When she went out to the fountain courtyard, she had all her money left from the market wrapped ready in a cloth to tip the captain. He had brought her such news.

The man was standing by the little fountain, looking down at the golden fish swimming about in the tank. For a ship's captain he was well dressed and very well groomed, his blond hair gleaming with cleanness in the spring sunshine.

When he looked up, she saw that he had grown as

pale as she had.

Clirando mastered herself.

"So, you're a liar, after all."

"No lies. By the gods, Cliro, trance or waking, I never lied to you once. And if I never wrote any love words upon the moon, I scarcely had time, did I? Or are you angry I delayed in finding you? For a while I could hardly even be certain you were real. By the hour I'd convinced myself, winter had closed the seas."

"I mean, Zem," she said, "you lied today, when you told them you were the captain of a ship."

"But I am. I'd sold my father's house, remember, and given up my legion. So… I bought a ship. What better means to come here? I've worked on ships before in my soldier's travels, I know them well enough. This one's a fine one. She's called *The Brown Warrior*. I named her after you with your tan skin and your acorn hair."

Clirando felt the yard, the town and the world draw far off from her. She stood in space, somewhere between sky and earth, and he stood facing her there, and they were alone together.

"Well," he said, "you helped save my mind and my soul on the Isle. But if I only *dreamed* you liked me, you must tell me to go. I warn you though—"

"You'll get drunk. Stay sober, Zemetrios. Stay with me."

He crossed the court in three strides and took her in his arms as she took him in hers.

They muttered into each other's mouths and necks and hair what lovers mutter at such times.

It had been an irony, he said, that as he set off to

seek her in Amnos, being one of the first ships out, it was he who ended up carrying with him the report of his own letter of her healing skills. As for her letter from Araitha, he was amazed when Clirando told him what it was.

He did not ask if she would ever seek for Araitha in the future. Nor did Clirando ask herself. The gods who had, it seemed, allowed all this, might one day advise her by some sign.

Four giggling novice priestesses, coming to feed the fish, dislodged the couple in the court.

So then they walked to her house down the winding streets.

Eshti showed great approval at the houseguest. "We shall have the best candles," she told them, "and the glass goblets from the chest."

"Eshti decides these things," said Clirando.

"So I see. That's good. It will leave you more time to concentrate on me."

"But when must you sail?"

"When I want. I'm my own man."

She thought, *he'll ride his ship across those treacherous seas, those waters of gales and drowning.* She thought, *we are both fighters. Neither can curb the other's life. The gods brought us together. Perhaps they will keep us together, now.*

The spring dusk came early. Up in the yard trees, the house doves were already arranging their nests. Which signified it would be a forward spring and summer.

When the candles were lit, the polished glasses filled, she sat with him and they ate supper as if they had done so for twenty years. Tonight, they would share the bed in her chamber. Where she had watched, sleepless, the unsleeping moon, now she would see him, and herself reflected in his gaze. Now she would see a future.

The sea wind tapped at the shutters, and the lamps before the household shrines dimmed and brightened. All the jewel-eyed gods there winked at Clirando and Zemetrios.

A trick of the light?

THE DRY SEASON

I

It was high summer when he came to Thraistum. There had been something of a ride, fifty miles of it, at a parade walk. The column of men and horses had marched its inexorable way through the opaque light of afternoon, the yellow dust going up like powdered biscuit. And along with the dust, the column carried its own weary clanking, the rumble of feet and wheels, the bitter reek of hot metal, raw leather stink and sweat stink. The baked clay road looked close to catching fire; the poplars at the roadside wafted an unslaked parchment smell. The kind of ride where you wanted water, not wine, at the end of it.

And Thraistum looked as if it had never seen water in all its days. The terracotta walls, flame-ringed by fields of tindery grain, the wretched red dwellings packed like cells in a hive. The fortress; built from rufus stone.

And he himself, Marsus Seteva, scorched bronze, shut in the armour of gilded iron, the lion's-blood cloak, thirty years old, and all his life a burning, of years, of hopes, of thought, of quietness. Never alone. Yet alone. Buckled into an iron shell and lost in a desert. His whole life, maybe, had been a ride like this ride to Thraistum. Predetermined, slow, without surprise. Without water.

"Does it never rain in this godforsaken place?" he asked the adjutant riding beside him.

"Oh yes, sir," said the adjutant, who was afraid of him, launching into a travelogue of the region. Which gods obtained where. When the harvest was. How the rain never fell till Novemia.

Of course, there was water in the water bottles, warm gritty slosh tasting of leather.

The other water, the waters of life, like that same tepid filthy stuff? Plenty of wine, naturally. Smoky taverns, red whores, smart army orgies, decorous dinners, wine and women cooled by snow, melted, the shade of furnaces. But no water. Not before. Not now.

And then.

Water.

The sombre papery trees had gathered themselves about a well. At the well a girl drawing up a vessel by a rope. Her arms were white, and her neck, amazingly white in the sun-glare. Her hair was loosely knotted on her head. Fine hair, the colour of—

Of water.

No colour, in fact, just sheen, burnish, reflection. And texture— it looked like spun silk. No. Spun water.

Back along the line a couple of men called to the girl at the well. Scorpius's voice came next, yammering them into muteness and awarding god knew what penalty for breach of discipline, marching as they were into Thraistum, the velvet-sheathed axe-blade of Remusa in this far-flung province.

But the girl seemed not to hear. She unbound the rope. She walked away from the well quietly, the vessel on her shoulder. The young girls here carried jars that way. The right shoulder. It meant they were virgin. He waited for the adjutant to tell him so, but the adjutant was silent.

Seteva turned his head slightly to watch her go down the slope carrying the virgin vessel. The poplar umbra splashed off her body like a wave. Suddenly she too turned and gazed straight at him, as if she felt his stare (the covert, leering stare, more likely, of half the column behind him). But she seemed to be looking at him. She had a strange expression. Almost of shock, but as if the shock had not yet reached her eyes, her lips, her physical surface. Her face was like the face of some alien creature, from another plane of existence. As though he had never seen a human face before.

So he recognised her. Infallibly. And equally infallibly, he, the leader of the column, was pushed onward by the column. Remorselessly on to the distant, redly bleeding town.

His oasis slid away. There had been no time to drink.

"I saw a girl I fancied, when I was riding in," he said idly over the sour wine to Cailo. "What are the local taboos like?"

"Variable. Where did you see her?"

"On the hill. By a well."

"There are always girls by wells," Cailo said, a bizarre apposition; but perhaps all he had intended was the domestic reference. "However, as it's the hill well…. There's a temple precinct a quarter of a mile down from the road. She'd probably be one of the girls from there."

Seteva smiled. The smile was arid. He was glad, and sickened. He'd been recalling only how she had carried the vessel, on the right shoulder.

"No," Cailo said, catching the smile, "the temple girls here aren't that kind. That's Tynt you're thinking of, and Eshtira, in the south. All sorts there. Girls on their backs, boys on their faces. Fun all around. But here. Didn't they tell you at Mareuna?"

"They didn't tell me much. One major god. Puberty rites for males. Monogamy. And – what is it? – the doves are sacred to the temple, so don't let the men take slingshots at them, despite descending guano."

Cailo nodded. "There's more. There's the sacrifice."

"Sacrifice?" Seteva repeated softly. He tried to go on grinning – doves spotting the valour of Remusa – but he saw flames curling out of a well.

"In five days' time. To make the rain come end-of-season."

"You mean an ox, or do these barbarians use horses?"

"Worse. I mean a girl. A temple girl, a virgin."

The fire ran into his mouth and through his belly.

"That's needlessly primitive, isn't it?" he said calmly. "Under Remusan rule, surely it gets stopped?"

"Hardly that. Come now, Marsus. You should know. The only thing that gets stopped under Remusan rule is failure to pay taxes. And insurrection. Remusa will tolerate anything else. Why not? Let the children play with their toys, as long as they're good children. And the Thraistians are models. Docile, friendly, courteous, hardworking. No problems here in twenty years. Their religion is the least we can let them have in return, if it keeps them so sweet. Come, it's not much to remember. Don't shoot the doves or shaft the temple girls. Sacrifice day is a festival. You'll probably be entertained by it. The town goes wild at sundown."

"And the girl? How do they choose? The shortest grass stem?"

"Not quite. It's an honour for her, actually, Marsus. That's how they see it. Die like this, and she's sure of her place in paradise. The same thing applies to their men who die in battle. Luckily, they don't go in for battles anymore. That sort of incentive makes men hell to fight, hell to kill. Fanatics. I'd rather combat wolves."

"When?" Seteva asked.

"When what? Oh, that. The girl – they choose her today, near sunset. Probably about the time you brought your men into the fort. They'd have been doing it then."

Seteva drank the last mouthful of liquid bitumen called wine.

He knew they had chosen the girl. Her life was going to be poured away on their altar, for their god.

It didn't matter.

Some slut.

Some dirty, foreign slut. Possibly a whore, for all the ritual chat. Virgin – what was that anymore? They'd sew them up again in half the markets of the world for two silver Remusan capitas.

Stupid slut.

"Have some more wine," said Cailo.

In the dark, crickets, and through the slit of window the dry stars flickered in the brazen black of the sky.

Soaked in heat, too parched even to sweat, he lay on his back on the straight hard pallet, thinking of fountains, lakes, oceans. Water.

Cailo rode out in the morning with his six hundred, going west to Mareuna.

The business of the fort was simple enough. Outside, the town was peculiarly tensed. Moving, working, going about its parochial affairs, but yet somehow poised and waiting. These were the Days of Salt, the period of purification before the sacrifice.

In four days' time they would give her to their god on the end of a knife.

Cailo had been definite: "You'd be advised to post men round the temple square. Not that they'll be necessary, but it's protocol. The temple building is to the north of the town; the square opens off three ways, closed on the temple side. A rotten area to contain in a skirmish, but fortunately you won't need to. They'll be gentle as lambs, and afterwards they get drunk, and the girls are generous to a fault. No taboos at all. Take my counsel and let the men off the leash. It does no harm, and they like babies here. You won't get recriminations."

"And if there are recriminations, you'll be in Remusa."

"Trouble at Thraistum is like the rain falling before Novemia. It never does. Just leave their religion alone, Marsus. The rest takes care of itself. This is going to be the nicest year of your army life. You'll go soft. Enjoy it."

The heat had drawn over like a curtain behind Cailo and the line of marching men and horses. Inside the curtain Thraistum cooked, and the dust lay like cinnamon on the air. The grain fields seemed to be smoking beneath the flat purple fresco of the hills, the blatant sky.

Days of salt. Salt in the wound. (A sword cut at Samaia, salt rubbed in at a makeshift hospital post, to staunch the bleeding; the smart searing to the bone, the backs of the ears, the groin, making him vomit with pain.)

The crickets had a different sound by day.

"Don't drink any water unless you mix it one-third with wine. It's not bad water exactly. Just native water. Full of red clay from the hills."

Cailo's imparted information had been comradely, endless.

He had a homily for every event.

The crickets tortured the grass.

The fortress should have been cool, its walls ten feet thick, in spots more. But the walls sweated and were not cool.

In the middle of the afternoon they brought the girl into the town from the hill precinct.

There were twenty priests, white linen and shaved heads, like the avatars of Aigum. There were subsidiary girls, too. They wore their hair long and unbound. In the middle of the procession two white she-asses pulled a little gilded car. The girl was in the car, motionless, and a child held a fringed sunshade over her head. The girl's hair too was unbound, plaited with flowers. Her wrists were ringed with silver, reminiscent of shackles.

Standing on the gate tower, he watched them pass through. People stood noiselessly in the street. The stillness had become symbolic.

He had the urge to shout.

Beneath the parasol, darkened, her hair appeared almost blue. She looked only before her. She did not seem afraid. Of course, she had been promised paradise.

Salt in the wound. It didn't matter.

II

"But I thought you spoke the language well," he said to the adjutant.

"Sufficient to barter, sir. To make myself plain. But not good enough for this, sir."

"Good enough? Where do you imagine we're going? The plaster-and-lathe temple of some crackpot god. Gloria Remusa, soldier. Remusans go where they wish and speak to whom they wish, in whatever manner they wish. It devolves on our subject peoples to learn our tongue; we do not learn theirs. Do you see?"

Seteva spoke in mockery of an attitude. The adjutant, missing, naturally, the mockery, tried to reason with him.

"Yes, sir. The priests do have an adequate command of Remine, sir. But for this—"

"This? What is so special?"

"There could be – misunderstandings."

"And so?"

"I took the liberty—"

"Did you," Seteva said.

The adjutant flushed. He said, "A caravaneer from Mareuna, versed in many languages. A rogue, but reliable if well paid. He's been supplying the garrison at Thraistum for years with – different commodities."

"I know the sort. All right. Where is he?"

The adjutant hurried out and came back with the caravaneer. Cailo had mentioned him, too, a tall, wiry swarthy man with a gold nugget in his left ear and oiled black curls springing across his shoulders under the wound head-cloth. He had bought Remusan citizenship and had donned a Remusan name to match.

"So you're Nylerus."

Nylerus bowed. His face held all the loving, compassionate wickedness of six generations of desert nomads commingled five generations more with the serpentine city folk of the East.

"The Kastor requires an interpreter. I am his servant."

"The Kastor is not certain he requires an interpreter."

Nylerus smiled, resting, as he did so, one long umber finger across his mouth, a parody of concealment. "The Kastor knows best. Gloria Remusa. But I speak Trasint as fluently as Remine. As my own tongue."

"Trasint?" Seteva inquired.

"The native name, sir, for Thraistum," the adjutant broke in nervously.

"What business brings you to Thraistum?" Seteva asked the Easterner casually.

Nylerus kept smiling. The smile said: Illegal and barely legal business. But you will comprehend that and pardon me. Remusans always comprehend how we second-class riffraff must scuff out our livings in this erroneous world. And we are quite useful to you, are we not?

"Goods to sell, as ever, noble Kastor. My party leaves in three days – the morning of the sacrifice, to be exact. I dare not risk my men in the town longer. On sacrifice night there is a festival, a riot. Thus, for three days, a portion less, my talents are at the worthy Kastor's disposal."

The temple was not as his mockery had fashioned it but a box of stone, older than the town, two or three centuries older than the fortress. A labyrinth of square courts opened into and out of each other. Daylight streamed in through high blue-painted walls, falling in spotlights, like static rain pools. It was actually cold, icy almost, coming in from the baked town.

Scorpius and ten polished privates kicked their heels in an anteroom. Seteva stood, helmet under arm, shivering slightly in the dank shade, politely waiting for the High Priest of Thraistum-Trasint to advance through the curtain. And at Seteva's side, Nylerus, the decorous servitor.

Religion had always been a focal point for danger and dissent. More focal than the subdued potentates, the petty kings. The princes of the temples had the bit of spiritual power between their teeth, and all over the Remusan-conquered world, High Priests were reckoned a cipher for trouble. *Save this one, apparently, in the backwoods of Thraistum. So why in the gods' name am I here, seeking to stir the dregs at the bottom of the cask?*

The curtain moved on its rings.

The High Priest entered.

He looked immediately at his visitor. The priest seemed to know Seteva, to recognise him. In late middle years, a heavy, rambling decline of manhood beside the fine-honed soldier, the High Priest of Trasint, like the temple itself, had built, nevertheless, upon the foundation of his age.

The priest bowed to Seteva. It was pure courtesy, neither fawning nor ironic. The bow accepted Remusa as master, accepted and ignored it. It was no matter. The sun still rose, the moon waxed and waned.

Seteva stood there, not acknowledging the bow. He addressed himself to Nylerus. "Tell him."

Nylerus spoke in Thraistian to the priest, conveying the thanks of the garrison's commander, Marsus Seteva, for the interview. This being also a device: formal words in one mode, the arrogance of the Remusan standing by, stone-faced, in another, as if disowning them.

Seteva watched the priest closely. To Nylerus, Seteva said, "Now tell him I want the sacrifice stopped."

Nylerus blinked. He made no remonstrance; the blink said it all. Delicately Nylerus translated for the High Priest.

The High Priest, too, looked nowhere but at Seteva. His face unchanged, he enunciated levelly to Seteva in the outlandish tongue. Seteva grasped a couple of fragments he could identify. The phrase that meant a betrayal, and the phrase that likened a man to a dog.

There was a brief lacuna.

"Well?" Seteva said, looking at the priest, addressing Nylerus.

"The Patriarch says the ceremony has always been permitted in the past."

"That's not what he said. Explain to the Patriarch that I don't allow any man to call me a scavenging cur. Even a priest."

The High Priest spoke mildly, in a sudden hesitant Remine: "That was not – decidedly – my meaning, Commander. My speech indicated – that even dogs cannot always obey their masters. We are – your dogs, Commander. But we cannot obey."

"You handle Remine excellently," said Seteva. "You should be able, therefore, to absorb my decision first-hand. I don't intend this rite to occur while I am in Thraistum. Offer your god a pig or a sheep. Your women have other uses."

Still mild, the priest said, "You do not know our ways, Commander. You must not expect to see sense in what you do not know. Under Remusa we have been allowed to follow our religion, always."

"As far as I am concerned," Seteva said, "to kill a woman on an altar is not merely barbarous, it poses a threat to law and order. While I am in command of the garrison, you will either suspend or discontinue the enterprise. That's my last word."

Now the priest stared. He uttered rapidly, once more in Trasint.

Nylerus said, "The Patriarch vows the rite cannot be put aside. That it is unavoidable. That he must risk Remusa's displeasure."

"Remind the priest that Remusa, displeased, has been known to nail men on crosses. And no priesthood was ever exempt."

Seteva turned; one stride would take him back through the outer doorway.

The priest said behind him, clear as a drop of water falling onto stone, "Commander, the girl is willing."

Seteva halted. "What did you say to me?"

"The girl is willing to die. I surmise this is what disturbs you, Commander. If you wish – with her own lips, she will assure you of the fact."

Seteva swallowed. Like an expert marksman the old man had pierced through officialdom, rage, Remusan arrogance, and struck the vital nerve. *I want to see the girl again. I want to hear her voice, touch her. I want to argue with her for her life, even though I can't do it in her own language. But. This is absurd.*

"The girl is nothing to me. Only a facet of your apparent refusal to abide by my order."

The priest spoke in Trasint.

"What does he say now?"

"Only that he is sorry, mighty Kastor, to offend you. And that the girl is in the adjacent courtyard."

It was becoming suggestive of a brothel, this insistence on the proximity of what he truly wanted. Except that, save in a very general way, that was not what he wanted. Nor what was offered.

Seteva's mouth was dry. A little breeze ruffled the linen curtain and he saw a pale shadow pass over it, outside. The girl?

As if mesmerised, he found himself crossing the room, drawing aside the curtain.

The court was half-open to the sky, white with sun to its centre, beyond that dyed blue by shade. There was a basin with static, transparent water in it. Doves were shooting up from about it like flung spears. The girl was seated on the lip of the basin.

She was combing her hair, slow shining motions, like waves running in over a smooth shore. There was no mark of death on her. Her stance conveyed a serenity of youth, gazing upon the endless vista of its future. That false dream of youth, which she, undeniably, could no longer possess.

Nylerus had reached him.

"No," Seteva said to him.

He moved out into the white sunlit half of the court and drove the curtain to with his fist as he passed, shutting the room into some other dimension that could neither see nor hear nor realise where he had gone, nor why.

The girl did not turn, but her hand with the comb sank away. Her hair was very long, covering her shoulders, falling like a silvery fringe almost into the water of the basin. Waterfall.

He walked towards her, around the basin. Her head was lowered, as if she examined the comb she held in her lap. The comb was ivory, bone, a mark of death after all. He could not see her face. He was the length of his arm from her when he spoke.

"Look up," he said. Perforce he used Remine, and she could not guess its meaning. But she did guess – the tone, perhaps – and raised her head.

Her eyes were wide and intent. Without modesty and without invitation, they explored him. He saw again that curious expression of amazement below the surface of her eyes. He could not explain to himself what she represented. His heart hitting his breastbone, the sound of blood in his ears like the sea, he thought, *Why did I never meet you on some marble avenue in*

Remusa, why did I never see you in some litter on the shoulders of slaves, going by, easy to follow? Why did I never meet you in the whorehouse at Tynt, easy to buy? Why not on the road to Mareuna, all those months kicking my heels, waiting for transport? Twenty, thirty girls, not one of them you. Why not that officer's wife at Samaia – I could have killed him. Easy, easy. But this. Why now?

She said something to him, softly, in Trasint.

"What?" he said, as softly. "I don't understand you."

She had risen. She held up her hand before him, palm open. It was the semantic tribal sign, current the whole earth over: *I am here without weapons.* Suddenly he fathomed what she meant, and, appalling him, his eyes stung with tears.

In Remine, concisely, a declaration she had learned, she murmured, "I have consented. To die. I will it."

"No." He caught himself struggling with the few bits of Thraistian he had acquired. "We – I – can prevent – this."

She only looked at him. Probably he had not said what he believed he had at all. Once more she said, gently, "But I consent."

"In gods' name," he said in Remine. In Trasint he sought and found the crucial word: "Why?"

Her eyes never left his face. She answered in Trasint, then in Remine she said: "There is no alternate way."

He could not offer the truth to her, gagged as he was, but he saw he did not need to. She knew, and in spite of the truth, she had said: There is no alternate way.

He turned only his head and shouted across the

court. "Nylerus!"

The doves swirled up again, white wings like segments of the white stone of the courtyard exploded by friction. Nylerus came from the curtained door mouth, through the swirling of the doves.

"Kastor?"

"Say to her that she is under the protection of Remusa. That no one is going to kill her."

Nylerus bowed and translated the sentences to the girl.

A veil seemed to slip down across her face.

She spoke in Trasint.

Nylerus said, "She replies that she is grateful, but it is not within your power to promise her this. She is not afraid, and she asks that you leave her in peace."

Nylerus did not smile now, too clever to smile at this ludicrous spectacle, the Remusan commander sent packing by the foreign child-woman. The gaze of Nylerus slid silkenly beneath its antimony, simply observing, as the Remusan swung abruptly about and walked out of the court. Quiet as sand or snake, Nylerus poured himself in the conqueror's wake.

Sentries patrolled along the ramparts of the fortress. Periodically the challenge rang out, isolated by the hot blue-black darkness, over the never-ceasing dazzle of the crickets. The stars burned inexhaustibly, and in the huddled, heat-swilled mass of dwellings below, the muddy lamps. Sometimes, from the northern end of the town, a dull vibratory chanting. The temple.

"Nylerus is outside, Commander."

Seteva glanced up. A pile of parchments lay on the

table before him, brown withered leaves, the business of the fort, unread. "All right."

Nylerus slipped into the room.

"I thought we'd paid for your services as interpreter."

"So you have, noble Kastor." Nylerus did not seem to note the parchments on the table, nor the wine jug. "I wonder if the Kastor will indulge me."

"I gather Cailo did. But I'm not Cailo."

"Indeed not, Commander. You must not suppose I expect a welcome at your fortress. Though I have been welcome."

"What do you want?"

"In the East..." Nylerus said. He had assumed a storyteller's voice. He looked a second at Seteva, to gauge his reaction. Seteva did not move. Nylerus rested his hands on the air, lightly, expressively. "In the East, our holy books inform us that when the first man had been made, the god breathed the divine breath into him, which became his soul, and caused him to become quick. It was then necessary to create woman. But the god did not breathe life directly into the woman. Instead he opened the man's body and removed from it a piece of the soul, and this he gave to the woman. Since then, for every man created, a piece of his soul is subtracted to quicken a woman. In memory of this deed the seed also passes from male to female. But if a man finds by chance the woman who contains that fraction of his own soul, he will know her, as he knows his own image in a mirror."

Outside something had caused the crickets to fall startlingly dumb.

"You gamble I have a weakness," Seteva said quietly. "You presume you can profit by it, just as you have profited here by Cailo's weaknesses."

"The Kastor misjudges me. Let me offer him the end of the story of the first man and the first woman who drew life from the same soul. Another god, jealous of the god who had quickened life in the bodies of men, seduced the woman. He put on the form of a serpent and persuaded her away by his beauty. They fashioned a second race between them, half-human and half-snake."

"From which, no doubt, you can claim descent."

"The Kastor is too generous. With my people the snake is revered for its wisdom."

"Then be wise, Nylerus. Get out."

"Before I go, Kastor, my caravan. It leaves on the morning of the sacrifice, one hour before the woman dies on the altar."

"You forget. The temple will forego the sacrifice, by my order."

"Oh, mighty Kastor—" Nylerus laughed, musically and low. "These barbarians... Do you think they will obey you? In preference to their god?"

"They will if they decide to keep their liberty."

"They are not civilised enough to put liberty before religion. This is your stumbling block."

The crickets had started up again, like flints perpetually striking on the peppery flanks of the hills.

Seteva poured himself wine. The jug was almost empty, and the liquor had the sour stale taste of repetition. "You'd better finish what you started to say to me."

"As the noble Kastor desires. I was about to postulate a theory. The men of my caravan – what are they? Villains, no more. The rubbish of the alleyways. And when they are in drink, gracious Kastor, neither god nor demon will deter them. Maybe they have seen a girl they fancy. What do they do? They abduct her, Kastor. They drag the poor wretch away with them, careless of whom she might belong to. And such a girl, once lost, is rarely recovered. For this cause I remove my caravan from Thraistum before the riotous celebration of the sacrifice is due. But possibly I am not quick enough. Possibly these dogs of mine have already espied some girl. Abductions can always be managed. Even a temple is not impregnable. And the priests. No match for jackals of the desert. There are a thousand crannies in these hills where such a theft might be hidden. I might detail for the noble Kastor the most likely concealments."

Seteva drained the cup and set it down among the parchments. "And the price?"

Nylerus touched one hand fleetingly to his brow, his heart. "To have the Kastor's friendship would be sufficient reward."

"I'm sorry to disappoint you," Seteva said. "I don't mean to be in your debt throughout the remainder of my time here. You've mistaken your man, Nylerus. Now, I can only reiterate my earlier proposal: Get out."

Nylerus bowed and moved towards the door. At the threshold he said, "On the day of the sacrifice, Kastor, I will leave thirteen men near the gate. They will be dressed in the manner of my people. You could not miss them, should you wish any service."

In the dark the crickets stopped again and again, for no obvious cause. Like a heart suddenly faltering. He remembered how his brother had died at Samaia, sliced in two, body bloodless, skin white as salt.

Salt in the wound.

Days of salt.

They had burned the dead at Samaia on one great pyre. The heat of it had spread like the heat of a summer day.

And the crickets began again. And again.

III

There was a woman in the town. She, or her Remusan clients, called her Pulcra, but she was ugly as forty years of whoring could make her. Her girls, younger, were a different matter.

In a minute cell of the scalding house, its walls painted with blue lotuses and red fruits, a girl the colour of amber took the wooden combs from her hair and the garish clothes from her body. They lay down on the pallet and made something, not love, between them. Fire, perhaps.

When he had had her, she offered him wine, politely lingering, eager to please. The wine was local, honeyed and thick, like syrup.

She spoke Remine haltingly but correctly. Anytime, she said, he would like her – or another girl, though she hoped it might be herself – they could come to him at the fort. There was a secret stair. Nylerus the Easterner knew the way. Jezit, the girl was named. The madam had told him. She would gladly come to him.

Any night, save tonight.

"Why not tonight?" he asked her. He wasn't interested, but the sight of her eased him, the small fluttery trained movements she gave, like those of a caged bird. Her accented, hesitant voice.

The light of day was already thickening like the wine. The dense coppery glare which preceded sunset.

"Tonight is the night of the Passage of Sin. She who is to die will sit before the temple. All who need may go by, touching her. Through the touch we receive blessing. She takes our sins upon herself. I have many sins."

"The men you couple with," he said noncommittally.

But she merely lowered her lids. "No. They are not my sins. It is no sin to couple."

"You'll have to find another formula, in any case. Has no one told you? There will be no sacrifice."

The girl looked afraid. She whispered something in Trasint and brushed at an amulet that had been glued between them on her breast all the time he lay over her.

In the narrow street the red rays of latter-day stained the clay houses. The commander of the garrison stood, partially anonymous in the casual wear of the fort, just a Remusan officer, his army cloak wrapped loosely about him against the heat.

His feet walked him northward, through the sweet stenches of dust, dung, and spice, the odour of the town at this hour.

What am I doing?

He waited for the sun to set, under the shadow of a

wall, across the temple square and facing towards the temple building. There was a matte blot on the light between him and the temple. It had not registered with him before. A stone slab about the height of a man, steps up to it, level across its surface.

No. This won't answer. I must have a reason for what I do. I have no reason. Nothing that has the guise of reason.

He had seen a man in one of the eastern villages five years ago. The man had run screaming through the village; he had eaten stones and drunk urine. When he uttered, it was gibberish. He was reckoned to be possessed by demons. That was, he had been motivated, without the power of his own will or sense, to perform acts injurious to himself and to others.

The sky altered from a wing of blood to a wing of indigo, and as the sky altered a crowd gathered along the edges of the square, as if the going of the sun had called it up.

Torches were flowing from the temple gate, droplets of fire running over the dusk.

There was no sound, no chanting. Voicelessly the crowd began to surge in on the gate, fulvously lit, then sinking forward into shadow.

The movements were such that he could not define their purpose.

Presently he also, muffled in the dark and in the cloak, joined the patient, slowly advancing crowd that pressed towards the gate.

Possessed.

By what?

A bit of his soul in her body. He had no soul; that was a dream of the East. The gods cared for a man simply while he was living. If there were gods.

Nobody stared at him or shrank aside disconcerted by this apparition of the Conqueror in their midst. They did not seem to notice.

Where the torches glared, he could see nothing. Only the silhouetted black shapes of men and women, shuffling, pausing, eddying away.

Then, like a curtain, the crowd parted. He beheld the light, and in the centre of the light, a creature in white robes, with a silver casque of hair; a blanched face, as if carved. A man knelt to her, contacting, with his fingertips, the hem of the robe, the silver- corded wrist. And next a woman, reaching to find the shoulder of the image. Sliding off into the shadow as the man had done, helplessly drawn to and thrust from the magnetic aura of the light.

It was the Remusan's turn now.

Take my sins. No. You are my sin, my stumble from the road of honour and duty. From sanity.

Did she remember him? The bleached face, white lips slightly parted, the eyes discs of jet, was raised to him like a mirror. But in the mirror nothing stirred.

There was a scent of incense and of drugs in the air.

He stood like a stone, a fold of his cloak over his head, hidden and unnamed.

The moment dissolved. Like a man stepping from a frieze, returned to flesh, he moved on into the shadow. Without touching her.

The girl, Jezit, sought him in the coal-black hour before dawn. Unsleeping, midway in the act of kindling the dish of oil, he heard a man laugh and a woman's protest. The sentry rapped on the door.

"One of Pulcra's daughters is here, Commander. She came in by the back stair and scratched at the postern." The man could barely restrain his amusement. Worse than Cailo, this new Kastor of the fort who could not leave the harlots alone.

Jezit poised in the dim yellow smudge of the lamp. Her head bowed, she extended to Seteva, mutely, a cloth-bound package.

"What's this?"

"It was sent to me, but for you, Kastor."

"And Nylerus reminded you of the way in? Don't use that stair again without my leave."

She did not reply, and he unwrapped the package, and there was the ivory comb the girl had plied in the temple courtyard, and wound about it, trapped in its teeth, a slender rivulet of colourless, shining hair.

His heart seemed to congeal. She had sent to him the symbol of her death. No speech could be so final or so essentially pathetic.

Like men drowning in some galley, casting their jewels from them, signets of their lives and office, to be swallowed by fish, perhaps, and discovered again a year later at the dinner table. His mother, when he was six years old, had recounted how his father's seal-ring had come back to her that way, from the sea battle at Mentum. But even then, somehow, he had known she lied, that the ring was a copy. That nothing, not even the glory of a name, could absolutely survive death.

The little whore drooped her head.

Let it end, he thought. *I'm far from land, but still the harbour is in sight. Turn back. She's nothing to you.*

Pretend, as her priests do, that you never ordered them to forego their sacrifice. These fools believed she died for them, their scapegoat. Too much hung on her death. She was condemned, for if she lived, their sins remained. Probably even the might of Remusa could not contain their spiritual panic and fury if they were cheated of their purging. He could not save her. But then, she was happy to die. Let her be happy. *One more death, what's that?* One more cup spilled on the ground.

He glanced at Jezit. "Well," he said. "Since you're here."

The hot shadows flared on the walls and sank, unappeased.

"It is a passing trouble," she said to him, consolingly, as if to a child. Doubtless she had seen men ashamed at their inability to fill her. He looked at the lamp glow and the quiescent shadows. The drought was not only in the world now, but within him. Dehydrated of water and of seed.

Die for me too, then, he thought. *Die for my sins, and give me back the rain, the water in the cup, my manhood and my soul.*

IV

"At noon," the adjutant said. "That's when they do it. To appease the sun, I think. Or to attract storms."

The hills seemed to be smoking. A brush of haze blurred the perimeter of the hard sky. Already the dust, momentarily laid by the flat black palm of night, was flouring the air, the ledges, the sills of the town, the sockets of the nostrils, eyes, and lips of men and beasts. Just another feverish day. This fifth day.

"I won't risk this mob getting out of hand," Seteva said. "Whatever precautions Cailo took, I want them doubled. Trebled, if necessary. A century deployed in blocks of ten, thirty men on each of the three open sides of the square, and ten across the gate."

"Yes, sir."

Scorpius cleared his throat. "That's extravagant, Commander."

"Not quite. Cailo treated this place as a combined brothel and sanctuary. It's neither."

Scorpius and the adjutant skimmed a glance between them, a memento of the harlot who had come in by the secret stair.

"And who's to take charge of this modest deployment, Commander?"

"I'll see to it myself."

And I'll see her die. But he was ready for that. He was balanced, beyond the trivia of his emotion, his superstition. Beyond the reach of her and the effluvia of this compost heap of barbarism and self-blindness. He walked at his own elbow. Inflexible, and objective. Guiding, indifferent.

"Where's that Easterner? Away yet?"

"Nylerus?" Scorpius spat economically through the window. "He rode out early. Though I hear he's left thirteen of his pack rats near the gate. Selling, or trying to sell, horses. No-one'll buy anything so close to the sacrifice. But, my god, who devised this system? A young, healthy girl to be butchered. Some decent farmer could have got sons on her. A waste, and no mistake."

"Pulcra could have found a use for her, at the very least," Seteva said.

They grinned, glad he would admit his weakness, reduce it thereby to the unimportant vice it was. The vice they thought it was.

Let from their cages, streamers of doves tangled across the cloudless sky.

The hundred men stood, sweating in their leather and iron. Scorpius, on the roan horse he had brought from Mareuna, sat by the temple gate.

The crowd pressed against the wall of shields and of Remusan soldiery. But hardly a sound came from the crowd. Once or twice a child, crying, was miraculously hushed. The dust was settling on the rims and folds and creases of the crowd, as if on statuary in a desert.

On his own face Seteva felt the pollen of the dust, while the black horse he rode became a grey dust horse.

He was tired, as if after a day's march. He ached, shut in the iron oven of heat and metal. His shadow lay on the ground under the hoofs of the horse. He wanted this to be over.

Inside the box of the temple a ram's horn moaned.

The gates swung open. From the well of shade into the bowl of sun, changing colour and texture as the sun struck them, the linen-robed priests, shaved like the avatars of Aigum, flickered black to white, black to white. A sharp perfume of myrrh fanned from their censers, penetrating the nasal passages, seeming to pierce the dome of the brain.

Like high tide they washed in about the stone slab in

the square, the slab that was the height of a man, steps up to it, level across its surface.

And now a girl came from the temple, also changing from black to white until, exposed in the force of noon, she too appeared to catch alight and to burn. She walked slowly, heavily, and observing her face, he saw that she was drugged, some poppy drink, to kill fear or to numb pain or simply to destroy the last vestige of the life-wish. She was very young. Life must be strong in her, despite her abnegation and her surrender to her god. She would need that drink.

He watched her face and felt nothing. She was a stranger, foreign-looking, not even actually beautiful. He could perceive now, as if from a high tower or across a vast distance, the gulf between them. She meant nothing. He was sorry for her, for her stupidity, for her death.

He had acted irrationally in this venture, and it could have become a worse irrationality if the more determined idiocy of these priests had not prevented it. He had been within an arm's length of losing everything. And gaining what? Some provincial doxy who could not even speak to him coherently in his own tongue.

Her eyes were entirely darkened by the drug, and nearly closed. Her heavy movements were graceful, sensual almost, as she moved towards the stone. As though she swam through a glaucous river.

Two priests drew her up the steps tenderly. Yes, most certainly, with tenderness.

Through the mask of the dust Seteva's mouth fixed itself in a sneer, and he was aware of the dust cracking to form new lines.

She lay on the slab, against the sky, the slight profile – head, breast, the curious addendum of the up-pointed, naked feet.

(He had seen enough of those feet, upturned, corpses in ranks, piled on each other, ready for burning after the battle.)

The ram's horn groaned again from the temple.

The fat High Priest was emerging now, and before him a girl about thirteen years old with a bough of greenery across her hands and something flashing white on that green, like a long blade of water.

Seteva was thirsty. The local wine wasn't bad, once you were used to it. And it would have to be wine. The local water had a foul taste.

The High Priest mounted the steps. He was on the other side of the slab, confronting Seteva over the profiled body of the girl. The thirteen-year-old offered the green bough to the priest, and he raised from it a honed and burnished knife, holding it aloft for the crowd to see, and perhaps for his god to see it, too.

It would require two cups of wine, more, to wash this dust-dryness out of the throat. *When I get to the fortress—*

He found, with a sort of unsurprised bewilderment, that he had kneed the horse and was riding forward. Not fast, in fact rather leisurely. The High Priest had seen him and had paused, the knife still pointed towards the sky. The priest's face was blank. Seteva felt the same blankness on his own face.

Now all the priests were in his way.

Suddenly he was no longer riding leisurely but with

a headlong violence. The linen-wrapped figures were toppling sideways, dividing, the slab loomed, horizontally spread with white, the fat middle-aged man beyond it, and the silver blade abruptly tearing the sky with its motion.

The blade in his own hand, which he had not been conscious of till that instant, sheared through the High Priest.

The man's face was red now with his own blood, bloodily washed of its blankness, whirling backwards—

Seteva pulled the white shape from the altar effortlessly. It was the first time he had touched her, but he did not think of it then, for she did not seem human, or real.

It was not quiet anymore.

He turned the horse, pulling on the bit to set the hoofs lashing, and plunged straight through the crowd. Women were screaming, and far off he heard, almost with nostalgia, the yammering yell of Scorpius. The soldiers had broken their formation. Seteva glimpsed three youths brawling over an armoured man on his knees in the dust, and the army sword spitting guts before the soldier went down. And he saw a woman scratching her cheeks and tugging out handfuls of her hair. And another soldier crawling in circles. And another dead. But these things seemed removed, at a vast distance, or perceived from a high tower.

He did not question his direction until he noticed the way unhindered before him, the town gate standing unbarred, a scoop of ochre light in the clay-red wall.

A sentry shouted from the wall as he clattered through, the white swath, which was a woman, clasped before him.

As the horse hit the wall of light beyond the wall of clay, men on horseback foamed around him.

"With us, Kastor!"

A second called in the eastern language, and Seteva identified the thirteen men Nylerus had left for his 'service'.

The striped head-cloths flapped over the black fleeces of hair, and the gems seared, a perfect component of this madness.

Seteva laughed, and all about the jackal teeth answered him, and the narrow eyes evaluated. They rode together, galloping for the hills.

The town sank in their wake.

He sat the part-dead horse, the senseless woman a leaden weight now on his arm. The sun had set, a sky the colour of apricots going out behind the land.

"Nylerus, I said," he repeated.

Despite their prologue of cries and the ride through the hills, they did not speak Remine, or would not. Nor did they appear to realise that their own leader was the man he sought in the encampment. Of course, he himself had no authority left with them, or with anyone. The insignia of Remusa all over him, the gilded armour, the lion's-blood cloak, the crested helmet, the bronze-hilted blade – each had become the silliest and most unsavoury kind of joke.

Yet he was not mad. It seemed quite reasonable, after all, that he should be here, with nothing, everything he had been reduced to a disaster and left behind him. Men he had known, whose lives were subject to his command, were scattered dead in that past. Reborn into chaos, only thus Marsus Seteva had entered the encampment in the hills. He had put himself into Nylerus's power as neatly as if Nylerus, some fictitious sorcerer of the East, had led him here. And now Nylerus was absent, the final tile left out of the wall. A chink in the reinvented, appalling structure of things as they had come to be. Strangely it was this, more than all else, which disturbed Seteva, provoking him to rage, so he shouted at the men about him: *Nylerus – Nylerus* – the only word they might logically be expected to grasp, but to which they refused to react.

Indeed, they had withdrawn from him, clearing a wide space about him as he sat there on the sodden horse, the white body of the girl leaden against his arm.

The sky faded, but the encampment fires rekindled the colour of the afterglow.

Nylerus stood by the horse.

His hands were raised as if to receive some burden from the soldier on his exhausted beast.

"Your men professed not to remember you, Nylerus."

"It was not that, Kastor. You made them uneasy."

"No longer 'Kastor,' Nylerus."

"No longer 'Kastor.' Dismount now; the ride is over. I will take the girl."

Seteva sat on the horse, looking at him. Seteva did not move. "Are there any women in your camp,

Nylerus? I think she'll need women to tend her. Women who speak her own tongue. I can still pay for the service, Nylerus. Remusan capitas."

"No, Kastor. That is no matter. This was not the service I offered, Kastor."

"Damn you, stop calling me that."

"As you wish, Marsus Seteva. But still it was not this service."

"What are you talking about?"

"I am saying to you, Marsus Seteva, that I offered you a method whereby you might bring your girl from Trasint before the sacrifice."

"Split hairs, Nylerus."

"Not so. Examine what you have brought from the town, Marsus Seteva. Closely."

The space had widened farther. Nylerus and the soldier and the horse and the limp form of the girl, ringed by fire-wash and shadow, by the settling canopy of darkness, by the men and their animals, but all a great way off.

He held her stiffly, like a heavy wooden bolster.

"They gave her a drug, to make her compliant," Seteva muttered. His arm no longer ached, holding her. His arm had grown into her body, become wooden as her body had become.

"She was compliant enough. Examine, Kastor. Examine."

Seteva glanced down.

Her face was tilted back, the bright hair gushing forth from the skull like spilling water from a tilted urn. Her eyes were open, dulled, opaque. Her lips did not meet. She stared at him as if about to speak.

A chill wind blew across the slopes, and the grass ran like the rollers of an ocean.

"Slow poison," Nylerus said softly, reciting to the lyre of the grass wind. "No harm in it, when they are to die anyway, their blood freed for the god. And it affords them a fair crossing from this earth into their paradise."

"She's dead," Seteva said.

"Yes, Kastor. From the moment she drank it. Dying even as she walked towards the stone. You cheated Trasint of her blood, but not of her death. Oh, they will not forgive it, Kastor. They will rebel and throw off the shackles Remusa put on them. Fresh soldiery will have to be sent to Thraistum. Men will need to be hanged, and crucified. Women raped. The temple burned. The fields salted. Afterwards, peace again. The peace of Remusa; quiescence beneath the booted heel. And you, Kastor, your own kind will hunt you like a dog. But all this is, ultimately, very little. Their god has what he desires. If he loves them, the rain will fall. The sun will rise. The moon will wax and wane. I am sorry, Marsus Seteva. I am sorry for you."

Seteva lowered the girl. Her bare feet met the grass of the hillside, and he let her go. She flopped like an emptied water sack, unhuman and spent, soulless, to the ground.

His arm, reprieved, began to pain him, prolonged runnels of pain flowing from the joints and sinews. He massaged the arm absently.

"What now?" Nylerus whispered to him.

"The end of the world," Seteva said. He pulled off the helmet of gilded iron, with its raw red comb, and dropped it by the white sack on the grass.

"Your world, Kastor."

"My world."

Seteva touched the horse, and tiredly, resignedly, it resumed the trained parade walk of the march.

"Wait," said Nylerus. "Where are you going?"

But horse and rider went by him, between the fires, and through the circle of firelit men, up the spine of one hill, descending from sight over another.

"The Remusan is going to Tophiteth, the place of burning," one of the men said malevolently. He spoke in the eastern language, his words striking on the quiet of the young night, scoring it like writing on a wall. "The Remusan is going to Hell."

About the Author

Tanith Lee (1947-2015) was born in London. Because her parents were professional dancers (ballroom, Latin American) and had to live where the work was, she attended a number of truly terrible schools, and didn't learn to read – she was also dyslectic – until almost age 8. And then only because her father taught her. This opened the world of books to her, and by 9 she was writing. After much better education at a grammar school, she went on to work in a library. This was followed by various other jobs – shop assistant, waitress, clerk – plus a year at art college when she was 25-26. In 1974, her career as a writer was launched, when DAW Books of America, under the leadership of Donald A. Wollheim, bought and published *The Birthgrave*, and thereafter 26 of her novels and collections.

Tanith was presented with a Lifetime Achievement Award in 2013, at World Fantasycon in Brighton. During her lifetime, she also received the World Horror Convention Grand Master Award, as well as the August Derleth Award and the World Fantasy Award for short fiction (twice).

In 1992, she married the writer-artist-photographer John Kaiine, her partner since 1987. They lived on the Sussex Weald, near the sea, in a house full of books and plants, and never without feline companions. She died at home in May 2015, after a long illness, continuing to work until a couple of weeks before her death.

Throughout her life, Tanith wrote around 100 books, and over 300 short stories. 4 of her radio plays were broadcast by the BBC; she also wrote 2 episodes (*Sarcophagus* and *Sand*) for the TV series *Blake's 7*. Her stories were read regularly on Radio 4 Extra. She was an inspiration to a generation of writers and her work was enormously influential within genre fiction – as it continues to be. She wrote in many styles, within and across many genres, including Horror, SF and Fantasy, Historical, Detective, Contemporary-Psychological, Children and Young Adult. Her preoccupation, though, was always people.

BOOKS BY TANITH LEE

Series

The Birthgrave Trilogy (The Birthgrave; Vazkor, son of Vazkor [published as Shadowfire in the UK], Quest for the White Witch)
The Blood Opera Sequence (Dark Dance; Personal Darkness; Darkness, I)
The Flat Earth Opus (Night's Master; Death's Master; Delusion's Master; Delirium's Mistress; Night's Sorceries)
The Lionwolf Trilogy (Cast a Bright Shadow; Here in Cold Hell; No Flame But Mine)
The Paradys Quartet (The Book of the Damned; The Book of the Beast; The Book of the Dead; The Book of the Mad)
The Venus Quartet (Faces Under Water; Saint Fire; A Bed of Earth; Venus Preserved)
The Vis Trilogy (The Storm Lord; Anackire; The White Serpent)
The FOUR-Bee Series (Don't Bite the Sun; Drinking Sapphire Wine)
The S.I.L.V.E.R. Series (Silver Metal Lover; Metallic Love)

Novels and Novellas

34
The Blood of Roses
Companions on the Road
Days of Grass
Death of the Day
Electric Forest
Elephantasm
Eva Fairdeath
The Gods Are Thirsty
Kill the Dead
Heart-Beast
A Heroine of the World
Louisa the Poisoner
Lycanthia
Madame Two Swords
Mortal Suns
Reigning Cats and Dogs
Sabella
Sung in Shadow
Vivia
Volkhavaar

When the Lights Go Out
White as Snow
The Winter Players

Young Adult and Children's Fiction

Animal Castle (picture book)
The Castle of Dark
The Claidi Journals (Law of the Wolf Tower; Wolf Star Rise, Queen of the Wolves, Wolf Wing)
The Dragon Hoard
East of Midnight
The Piratica Novels (Piratica 1; Piratica 2; Piratica 3)
Prince on a White Horse
Princess Hynchatti and Other Surprises
Shon the Taken
The Unicorn Trilogy (Black Unicorn; Gold Unicorn; Red Unicorn)
The Voyage of the Bassett: Islands in the Sky

Story Collections

Blood 20
Cold Grey Stones
Colder Greyer Stones
Cyrion
Dancing in the Fire
Disturbed by Her Song
Dreams of Dark and Light
Fatal Women
Forests of the Night
The Gorgon
Hunting the Shadows
Nightshades
Phantasya
Red as Blood – Tales from the Sisters Grimmer
Redder Than Blood
Sounds and Furies
Tamastara, or the Indian Nights
Space is Just a Starry Night
Tempting the Gods
Unsilent Night
Women as Demons

TANITH LEE TITLES PUBLISHED BY IMMANION PRESS

The Colouring Book Series

Cruel Pink
Greyglass
To Indigo
Ivoria
Killing Violets
L'Amber
Turquoiselle

The Blood Opera Sequence

Dark Dance
Personal Darkness
Darkness, I

Novels and Novellas

34
Ghosteria Volume 2: The Novel: Zircons May Be Mistaken
Madame Two Swords
Vivia
The Heart of the Moon

Collections

Animate Objects
A Different City
Ghosteria Volume 1: The Stories
Legenda Maris
The Weird Tales of Tanith Lee
Venus Burning: Realms: Collected Short Stories from 'Realms of Fantasy'
Strindberg's Ghost Sonata and Other Uncollected Tales
Love in a Time of Dragons and Other Rare Tales
A Wolf at the Door and Other Rare Tales

Of Interest to Tanith Lee Enthusiasts…

Night's Nieces

This anthology is a tribute to Tanith Lee, comprising short stories written shortly after her death by some of her writer friends to whom Tanith was a profound influence and inspiration: Storm Constantine, Cecilia Dart-Thornton, Vera Nazarian, Sarah Singleton, Kari Sperring, Sam Stone, Freda Warrington and Liz Williams. With an introduction by Tanith's husband, the artist John Kaiine. Illustrated throughout by the contributors and with photographs from Tanith Lee's personal collection.

IMMANION PRESS

Purveyors of Speculative Fiction

A Wolf at the Door by Tanith Lee

Includes 13 tales, most of which appeared only in magazines or rare anthologies. 'A wolf at the door' implies hidden threat – until the door is open, we don't really know what's out there. And now the beast is upon you, scratching at the wood, its hot breath steaming on the step. Will you survive the encounter? Perhaps, once the door is opened, what you might have thought to be a threat turns out to be something else entirely. But of course, it can also be a werewolf…
ISBN 978-1-912815-04-3, £11.99, $15.99 pbk

Breathe, My Shadow by Storm Constantine

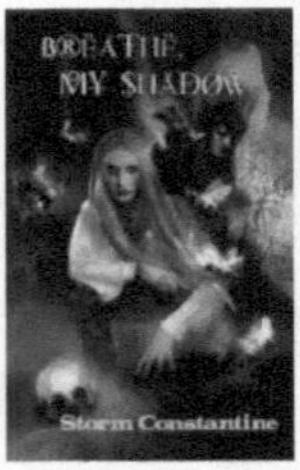

A standalone Wraeththu Mythos novel. Seladris believes he carries a curse making him a danger to any who know him. Now a new job brings him to Ferelithia, the town known as the Pearl of Almagabra. But Ferelithia conceals a dark past, which is leaking into the present. In the strange old house, Inglefey, Seladris tries to deal with hauntings of his own and his new environment, until fate leads him to the cottage on the shore where the shaman Meladriel works his magic. Has Seladris been drawn to Ferelithia to help Meladriel repel a malevolent present or is he simply part of the evil that now threatens the town?
ISBN: 978-1-912815-06-7 £13.99, $17.99 pbk

The Lord of the Looking Glass by Fiona McGavin

The author has an extraordinary talent for taking genre tropes and turning them around into something completely new, playing deftly with topsy-turvy relationships between supernatural creatures and people of the real world. 'Post Garden Centre Blues' reveals an unusual relationship between taker and taken in a twist of the changeling myth. 'A Tale from the End of the World' takes the reader into her developing mythos of a post-apocalyptic world, which is bizarre, Gothic and steampunk all at once. Following in the tradition of exemplary short story writers like Tanith Lee and Liz Williams, Fiona has a vivid style of writing that brings intriguing new visions to fantasy, horror and science fiction. ISBN: 978-1-907737-99-2, £11.99, $17.50 pbk

www.immanion-press.com
info@immanion-press.com

www.ingramcontent.com/pod-product-compliance
Lightning Source LLC
Chambersburg PA
CBHW051301250626
47155CB00009B/3383